THE BEST PEOPLE

ALSO BY ROBERT LOPEZ

Part of the World

Kamby Bolongo Mean River

Asunder

Good People

All Back Full

A Better Class of People

Dispatches from Puetro Nowhere

THE BEST PEOPLE

— a novel in stories —

Robert Lopez

2580 Craig Rd.
Ann Arbor, MI 48103
www.dzancbooks.org

Library of Congress Cataloging-in-Publication Data Available Upon Request

ISBN: 978-1-938603-24-2
First US edition: April 2025
Interior design by Michelle Dotter
Jacket design by Steven Seighman

Printed in the United States of America

10 9 8 7 6 5 4 3 2 1

THE BEST PEOPLE

First Draft

DON'T GET BORN, don't be a person, don't get born as a person to a family of people. Don't be black or white or brown and don't be short or fat or skinny. Don't be a brother or sister or cousin or uncle or mother or father. Don't go to school or get a job or consult with colleagues or attend meetings. Never sit at a table where other people are already seated.

Full Stop

I WANT TO HAVE SEX with someone, a person. It could be a man or it could be a woman or it could be a man who was once a woman or a woman who was once a man or someone who is both all the time and every day. The person could be ugly or pretty or have no looks at all. I said this to my sister the other day and then I added the words *full stop* for emphasis, which means there's nothing else to say on the subject and I don't want to hear it. The way it sounded was the person could be ugly or pretty or have no looks at all full stop. I said they can be a walking piece of paper or they don't have to walk even one step, they can be immobile, bedridden. I don't need for someone to be ambulatory to have sex. I don't care about age or race or color or creed or how tall or short the person is or how fat, either. I don't care if they have a clubfoot or a trick knee. I don't care if they have a widow's peak or plantar wart. They can be walleyed or cross-eyed or cockeyed. I want to have sex with someone who is sucking in oxygen and blowing out carbon dioxide. This is when Sister said something crass in response. Sister can be like that full stop. This is why I've decided to stop talking to Sister, who was busy doing the dishes in cold water but it never works out because the dishes never come clean. The way we divide the housework is I do the cooking and maintenance and she does the housekeeping which means we live in squalor. This is when Sister said, what about me, what about what I want, and I can't even mention what she wants because it's awful. I told her that she needed to take a hard look at herself starting right now. This is when Sister took a pot of boiling water off the stove, said don't think I won't, and stared me down. People shouldn't have to live like this so you can't blame me for anything I might say or do moving forward, particularly when it comes to Sister. I decided to keep talking because I had a point to make and I didn't think Sister would try to scald me again after what happened last time, so I said I want consent but after consent is given they can lapse into a coma. I can say, do you consent to sex and they can say yes, and I can say if you lapse into a coma can I keep going and if they say yes then we'll be right for each other. I know Sister didn't hear me say that because she walked away from the sink and threw a dish at the wall and then slammed a door for emphasis. She can stay behind a slammed door for days at a time, and I revel in the quiet whenever she does. Maybe if I get to have sex I can forget about Sister for a while and wouldn't that be nice. I need to prepare for all eventualities, for sex with some kind of person and the subsequent disappointment and fear and resentment and death. I want to be ready for regret. I want the person to know they can continue the sex with me should I die in the effort. Death shouldn't slow either of us down, not for half a step. Nothing at all should slow us down, not even the sky falling all around us. If Sister were in the same room she'd say something crass about this, too, which is why whenever I talk to Sister I wonder why I bother but she is the only other person here so I have no choice. But that doesn't mean I want her to talk back because when I'm talking the other person should listen and remain quiet. So, Sister, even after I die in the effort there should be urgency and dread, the desperate commingling, the push and pull, give and go, stick and move. Me and the other someone who is a person and it could be early in the morning or late at night or high noon on a Tuesday. The weather can rain or snow or sleet or hail or hurricane or tornado. I want to have sex with someone that's a person in the world, utilizing every part of our bodies so that maybe our souls connect on an astral plane, and I don't want to hear anything else about it, Sister, full stop.

If You Make the Mistake

If you make the mistake of being born do not compound it by surviving past childhood. Everything after childhood will be a profound disappointment to you and everyone you know. Your education will be a disappointment and your job will be a disappointment and your love life will be a disappointment. Your friends will also disappoint you. That day you and Sister built a snow fort in the backyard and didn't allow your cousin to help with its construction or enter after its completion and every time he approached, the two of you pelted him with snowballs until your grandmother came out in the freezing cold wearing only a housecoat to give everyone in the world what for should be the last thing you ever do.

An Attempt at Sex

THE MAN IS TRYING to have sex with the woman. This is the second time he has tried to have sex with this same woman, but he can't remember when they first tried. He does remember they were at her place, in her apartment, and it was warm. He was sweating and mopping his brow with a handkerchief. He regretted not inviting the woman over to his place where he has two air conditioners running continuously from May through October. He knows better than to accept invitations during the summer months but sometimes he forgets when it comes to women and the possibility of sex. He'd asked the woman if she had an air conditioner or electric fan, perhaps one that oscillated. She said she had neither and that she was sorry. He didn't believe her. It was how she pronounced the word, drawing out the second syllable as if she were mocking him. He said what kind of a person goes through life without an air conditioner or electric fan and immediately regretted it. She didn't answer; instead she crossed over to the other side of the living room to retrieve a drinking glass. Then she removed a pitcher from the refrigerator and filled it with water. She took a drink from it, staring directly at him as she did. He didn't know what to do with himself, so he did nothing. He stood upright and tried smiling but it felt unnatural so he turned his attention to the window. There was nothing to look at except another apartment building across a short alleyway. He saw falling drops of water, condensation from an air conditioner. It looked like ice melting. For a second he thought of a glacier, the polar ice caps. He imagined fetid puddles on the ground and the sound of a dripping faucet. He imagined rising sea levels and emaciated polar bears.

He thought maybe this reminded him of a similar encounter. Standing upright in a stranger's kitchen, sweating, not knowing where to put his hands, not knowing if he should excuse himself and go home. This was one of the concerns of aging, he decided, that everything seemed like a repeat, like there was no new content and his own life was cancelled years ago and not even running in syndication anymore. Lately he has wondered if he's lived too long or if he should've done something else with his life. Maybe he should've married someone and this way he wouldn't be trying to have sex with this woman for the second time. There is something undignified about a middle-aged man trying to have sex with a much younger woman, but perhaps he's wrong about this, too. He's not sure what to think or what to do with his hands, so he puts them in his pockets but then decides it's too hot for his hands to be buried inside pockets. He relocates his hands to the back of his head as if he's about to do a sit-up. He doesn't think he'd be the sort of married man who would cheat on his wife, but he probably is that sort.

Later in the evening, before they tried to have sex, she showed him her new tattoo. She called it an ambigram, which was a term he'd never heard. The tattoo spelled out *I'm fine* or *Save Me* depending on how you looked at it and he thought it clever, but he wasn't especially interested in tattoos and didn't consider them attractive on a woman. It didn't matter because he knew the tattoo wouldn't stop him from having sex, as it wasn't a turnoff like being wall-eyed or cross-eyed. That is, if sex was still a possibility. He wasn't sure anymore given his comment about the lack of air conditioning and he wasn't sure he cared. He'd had sex with two other women last week and neither encounter was satisfying.

He remembers asking to shower before they tried to have sex because he'd been sweating and he doesn't like to sweat unless he's playing tennis, which he does four or five times a week. Tomorrow he is slated to play mixed doubles with Manny and two women he hasn't met, but he isn't thinking about this now.

She didn't think he was serious about wanting to take a shower. She said, you're asking to take a shower and he said, yes I am. She said, you're serious. He said, I am indeed. She walked down the hall and fetched him a fresh towel from the linen closet in her bedroom and then directed him to the shower. She said, you have to pull the handle out and turn it all the way to the left if you want the water hot. He thanked her, tried to make a joke about the absurdity of this request, and disrobed. He made sure to soap himself thoroughly and quickly, as he didn't want to keep the woman waiting. Otherwise, he enjoys long showers and can spend upward of thirty minutes inside one. He doesn't listen to music in the shower but he would if he had some kind of sound system or speaker inside or near the bathroom. Years ago he had what was referred to as a boom box, but he never called it that. He never shaves in the shower and doesn't understand why any man would shave in the shower instead of in front of a mirror and over a sink. He never masturbates in the shower, as he doesn't like to masturbate standing up. He never urinates in the shower, though he almost always has to urinate. He thinks there is something wrong with his bladder or kidneys. He hasn't been to the doctor because he doesn't trust doctors and he doesn't want to find out he has cancer.

He never takes a bath, though sometimes he wishes he were the sort of person who could take baths. Instead, he stands himself up in the shower and mindlessly rotates his body around and around and lets the spray wash over him as he thinks about whatever is troubling him. Frequently he will think about death, his own death and the deaths of family members and friends. He also thinks about his local sports teams or a potential romantic interest, if he has one. If he doesn't have a current romantic interest he tries to figure out ways to cultivate such. He thinks about his friends and which of them might have another friend who is single and looking to date. Sometimes he'll think about women he has been involved with, but he never wonders what their lives are like now. Thus he doesn't know that the woman he dated for six months over twenty years ago is undergoing her final round of chemotherapy for non-Hodgkin's lymphoma. He doesn't know that she will die from complications next year, surrounded by her friends and family. This woman he remembers as Sofia, but her name was Esperanza. She talked out of the left side of her mouth, as if she were trying to keep what she said secret from her own right ear. She wore four or five earrings in each one. Two equally small hoops and a variety of silver studs that trailed down her lobes like tracks. If he remembers anything about her this is what he remembers.

He also rarely thinks about the actress he dated and who claimed she was pregnant shortly after they started sleeping together. He couldn't understand how she could be pregnant when they'd had the sex in question a day after her period had concluded. He had asked her beforehand if they were safe and she indicated that they were. He thought it was some sort of trap, a scam, like those he'd seen on television or in the movies. He was about to break it off with her as there was no sexual chemistry and perhaps she sensed this so she made up the story about being pregnant. Having sex with the actress was like making love to an aquatic mammal that just died. The body was still warm, but totally unresponsive. During this time he sought out the counsel of trusted friends, who advised him according to their own experiences. One friend, a colleague and father himself, told him that if she was pregnant, and he was, in fact, the father, it would be the greatest thing that ever happened to him. He said that he'd love this child in a way that is unfathomable to him now. The man doubted he would feel this way, but allowed for it as a theoretical possibility. But still, the man didn't like children, found them to be tedious and petulant. Another friend, a woman, said he shouldn't trust any woman nearing forty when it comes to birth control. This he vowed to keep in mind regardless of whether he was about to become a father or not. He'd planned to cut off communication with the actress and wait it out. In seven or eight months, he'd stalk her workplace to see if she were showing. If he were the father he would do the right thing, which he figured amounted to child support. He anticipated having to take a paternity test at some point, but months later she claimed she'd had a miscarriage and said he should never contact her again.

That night, however, in the shower, he was not thinking about any of this. He remembered to squeegee himself before using the towel as another ex-girlfriend used to complain that he made the towels too wet after use. She'd complain about the smell of mildew in her bathroom whenever he was over. This night he emerged from the bathroom wrapped in the towel, which was damp but not soaked through, after showering for only five minutes. The woman remained fully clothed, wearing jean shorts and a tank top, while reading a magazine in the living room. He sat down next to her and she pretended not to notice. She kept on reading her magazine, and so the man picked up another magazine from the coffee table and started to page through it. This went on for almost a minute before they both laughed. This is when they tried to have sex for the first time, which had to have been last summer or the summer before last.

He has known this woman for three years but this is only the second time he has tried to have sex with her. The first time resulted in abject failure. They could not achieve congress, let alone intercourse. The problem was he couldn't get aroused, which, now that it comes back to him, isn't true. He couldn't sustain an erection is what actually happened. He'd have an erection for a minute or so but then he would lose it. This is when he'd go through the machinations of getting the erection to return, which it did at least two or three times, but each time it subsided yet again. This had never happened to him before and he thought of it as an anomaly. Something wasn't right between the two of them. There was desire, probably, and interest and curiosity, but also trepidation and fear. The man didn't feel trepidation or fear, but he sensed the woman did. She held her body rigid, as though she were doing yoga or isometrics while he kissed her belly or massaged her buttocks. He stopped every so often and asked, is this okay or does this feel good. Most of the time she said nothing. Once or twice she said, yes, it's fine. The way she said this made the man think it wasn't fine, that it wasn't enjoyable. This is why he couldn't sustain an erection. He remembers mopping his forehead with the bedsheet while trying to get his erection back. He remembers hoping she didn't see him mopping his forehead with the bedsheet. She had her eyes closed the entire time, from when he first started kissing her and pulling off her tank top and jean shorts. Finally, after too many attempts, they gave up. He collapsed next to her as she pulled the sweat-stained bedsheet over her naked body. It seemed as though she were pulling her legs up and into her chest, like she was trying to fold herself up before putting herself away.

Neither the man nor the woman said anything for a minute. The man spent this time trying to puzzle the entire interaction out, from beginning to end. He always thought he could perform sex irrespective of any external factors, though one's partner being petrified probably didn't qualify. Perhaps it was a lack of chemistry, though that didn't make sense. There was always sexual tension in their encounters and exchanges. It was unmistakable, though perhaps he was mistaken. Perhaps what he perceived as sexual tension was simply awkwardness and confusion. Then the man said, next time it will be easier. He said, it's normal for this to happen the first time people try to have sex with each other. They're nervous and awkward and only starting to get to know each other, what each person likes and dislikes. She said, I'm sure you're right. He remembered seeing similar scenes in television shows and movies where the man couldn't perform and was rendered impotent. He remembered the man feeling embarrassed and apologizing to his cohort for being unable to perform. The man in the television show or movie said something about this never happening before but he knew better than to say that. She'd take it the wrong way, which also isn't true. She'd get offended is more accurate, but she would be taking it the exact right way. He figured he should apologize because he didn't want the woman to think there was something wrong with her, that it was her fault. So he apologized, though he knew that he was blameless. He'd spent a substantial amount of time on his standard foreplay maneuvers, which were comprehensive and often enjoyed by his partners. There was only one partner who seemed unaffected and disinterested in these efforts and that was maybe twenty years ago. Her name was Esperanza or Sofia and he remembers that he was twenty-six and she was in her mid-forties or even older. At the time he was excited by this disparity in age, but now that he is almost fifty this is no longer the case. This Sofia's hair was thick and dry to the touch, but it was long and he's always liked long hair on a woman. Her feet were bony and misshapen and so the man left them alone. The best part about her was that one leg was longer than the other and she had to wear corrective shoes to keep herself upright and ambulatory. She told him she was once bedridden for two years and the worst part about it were the sores. The skin on her stomach was flaccid and featured stretch marks, which he'd never seen before. He asked if she'd had children but she answered no. He chose to believe her because he didn't care, but the woman was lying. This Esperanza had two grown children, one who worked as a dental hygienist and the other a senior in a liberal arts college in the Midwest. Both will be at her bedside next year when she finally succumbs to complications from non-Hodgkin's lymphoma. Regardless, Sofia seemed bored when he worked her nipples or whenever he put his mouth anywhere on her, including her clitoris. She held herself rigid and made no sounds, very like the woman with whom he is presently trying to have sex. But the man is not thinking about Esperanza or Sofia and hasn't for years. This night the man wanted the woman to feel desired and appreciated. He couldn't tell if she had to spend time fending off an army of suitors. He remembers hearing a friend of a friend say something like *there will always be suitors* during a discussion about dating, but that couldn't be every woman's experience. The woman with whom he is trying to have sex is attractive to him but perhaps not to others.

He genuinely believed that next time would be better. She would feel more comfortable and could relax and enjoy herself, and it turns out next time is now, a year or two after the first time, in her apartment again. In the interim the man has had sex with several women and almost every attempt was successful. Which isn't to say that all parties achieved orgasm every single time, but there was congress and intercourse and the requisite thrusting to and fro. There was tenderness and passion and carnality and boredom. There was the routine collapsing on the bed from exhaustion, fulfillment, or resignation after it was over. The man doesn't know if the woman has had sex in the interim and he doesn't want to know. He feels this way every time a friend or acquaintance or colleague betroths herself to anyone who isn't him. He thinks of it as a betrayal and he knows it is ridiculous of him to think this way, which is why he doesn't want to consider whether the woman has had sex since last they'd tried together. Either answer would be disappointing. If he finds her attractive it's likely she's captured the interest and attention of other men, and it seems natural that she might've been attracted to or interested in a man at the same time but he can't know for sure. He doesn't know if she'd behave the same way with another man, but he suspects she would. She'd be nervous and uncomfortable and seem distant and hold herself rigid and the man would have to be made of something other than flesh not to be affected by it.

The Best People

If you make the mistake of conversation, do not ask or answer personal questions. Speak only of the weather and how awful it is. How one day it's too hot and the next day too cold. Talk about the time you watched a tornado blow past your living room window. How the day went yellow and quiet before it happened. How the rain came down sideways and the trees were bent into unnatural shapes. How you walked the streets after it was over to survey the damage. How everyone was outside doing likewise. How so many trees were uprooted, how they smashed through cars, how they blocked traffic. How it was the only time you ever saw what was underneath a tree.

A Town Called Luck

Manny told us it was a free-for-all and we believed him. We always believed what Manny told us, and this business with the free-for-all was no different. A couple of years ago Manny told us about daylight savings time and how it was a sham and had nothing to do with the farmers. He said it was a government conspiracy, something about the deep state. Manny was also right about the polar ice caps and the sky falling down and how you shouldn't drink milk once you've reached adulthood. He said, I ain't had no milk and butter since that cow's been gone and we didn't know what he was talking about. He said he'd discovered a new use for electric fans, that he could control the weather with one so long as it was at least four feet tall. He said it had to do with atmospheric pressure and the rate of oscillation. We couldn't follow what he was saying but that wasn't unusual. He said if we understood chaos theory or fractal geometry then we'd understand. This is one of the reasons he hated when we had to move the clocks back and forth, because it didn't align with the tenets of space time or metaphysical duality. He would say, what was so good about daylight anyway, and he was right. Someone said daylight was the best disinfectant but Manny said malarkey. He said it was sunlight, that sunlight was the best disinfectant, and then he said white vinegar was better than either. He said white vinegar was the best cleaning solvent in the world and that it's always important to keep clean. Manny said the world was a filthy place and the air was filthy and the ground was filthy and the people were even filthier. Then someone said what's the difference between daylight and sunlight and Manny said, I can't believe they let you outside. Everyone stayed quiet for a minute, and then Manny walked away shaking his head. We could tell he was disappointed. We didn't blame him because we were disappointed in ourselves.

We also don't blame Manny for this business with the free-for-all. Manny had seen more than his share of free-for-alls and we knew that going in. He grew up that way, what with his mother and father. They used to keep him out back in a shed, fed him only rice and beans and would beat him with a nightstick. He said it wasn't as bad as it sounds and because he said it we believed him. He used the phrase, time without number, to talk about how many free-for-alls he'd witnessed. He said a good free-for-all attracts the best people and we weren't sure if he meant us. We figured he was referencing someone else and so we waited for reinforcements. We knew we needed help and kept a lookout for anyone who might be on the way. Maybe we are still waiting. But while we wait we think about what we've done wrong and how we can do better. We always wanted Manny to think of us as the best people, but by the time we got there the cops had the whole area cordoned off and Manny was nowhere to be found. Right after that they hauled everyone off to the clink and sat us down in rooms with no windows and bad lighting. They asked us questions about Manny, how we knew him, where he liked to go at night, if he was born in this country. They told us we shouldn't leave town, that if we heard from Manny we were to call them at once. They kept after us for two days before they let everyone go. It was something like police brutality, which is another thing Manny told us about. All of us had to shield our eyes for the sun when we stepped outside, and it was like we were blind for a few minutes. We had to wander around the parking lot for an hour as we regained our senses. But all of this is beside the point, and maybe even a waste of time. All we want to say is that if Manny is out there somewhere, if he's still alive, that he should be proud of us and know in his bones that we are indeed the best people, because we told them nothing and never will.

A Church by Daylight

THE SKY IS NOT UP in the sky and the moon is no longer a moon and there are no trees or dogs or electric fans or kitchenware and there is no daylight savings time because there is no daylight to save.

What Water Does to Wood

My FATHER SAID there was something bad wrong with me, claimed I was a slowdown on the uptake, that I'd best learn a trade and right quick. I always stared at his boots when he talked at me like this, which were always scuffed and mud-soaked and had a .38 Special tucked deep inside the right one. Every time it looked as though he'd fled the scene of an unspeakable crime.

He said I never gave him cause to dispute the notion, that there was something bad wrong, not once in the fourteen years we were associated.

My mother never had much to say on the subject, though I believe she stood tall in agreement. She was always off to the side or behind my father, sometimes making faces, sometimes pointing to the ceiling for emphasis.

My mother would speak in tongues, which I believe was intended to either scare or comfort me. I never could understand what she said, not a single word or sound.

I haven't seen either in years, don't know if they are alive and well or dead and buried or any combination of those.

The upshot is my father was right. I lose consciousness about twice a day and always at an inopportune time. It has to do with there's not enough oxygen feeding the brain. One of the doctors called it a coughing syncope, but that never sounded right to me.

I'm sure it's a cancer, but I don't know from what part of my body or if it matters.

Also, I have psoriasis, but it isn't moderate to severe like my parents had.

There were trees along the wayside and people walking dogs and themselves for exercise when I came to this last time.

I don't know for how long I was under.

I remember that up in the everywhere sky clouds rolled past and on the ground it was tumbleweeds. I remember something like a whirlwind or tornado.

This is how I came to Luck, how I fell with a thud.

I had a bad knee or a broken heart, no job, and some real troubles.

I've been here ever since, though wherever here is I cannot feature. I think it's Luck, but it could be anywhere in the civilized world or America. I can't see anything distinguishable from where I lie prone on the ground.

I'm not one to point fingers, but if I had to I'd lay blame with my mother and father, who kept me sequester-like in a back room that had no windows or heat or electrical capacity. One or the other would come by every few days to check on me, feed me rice and beans. They put newspapers down on the ground for my facilities.

This is how I learned to read some, which is how I tried to pass time, which I could never tell because I had no clock, watch, or calendar.

Otherwise, I'd listen to the rain or my mother and father going about the business of connubial bliss. They mostly kept to themselves, never had people over to mix drinks with them.

I thought I heard other children carrying on at night, thought maybe they were being held in a back room on the other side of the house, but maybe it was a television or radio program.

This is also when I learned what water does to wood.

What water does to wood is it rots it out and allows the formation of mold and it's the mold that compromises your pulmonary capabilities.

What water does to wood is it gives you emphysema, which is probably another form of cancer.

The doctor said this is what I have now, said it was chronic. He said I'd have to take it easy for the rest of my life and that I shouldn't buy any green bananas.

That back room at my parents' house was an add-on so they could keep me away from the rest of them. I think maybe I did have a brother and sister because I remember my parents making remarks I couldn't understand, about a little girl who had a club foot and plantar wart, but I never met anyone formally.

Only my mother and father came to visit me in the back room, which they built together out of plywood and spite.

Out here I've got a knapsack I use as a pillow and an old Army jacket for a blanket.

What's bad is I have a hard time walking on account of my knee. Also, my boots, which are old and the soles are worn down to paper thin. I always slip on the ice and fall down for lack of traction.

My mother and father took turns beating me with a nightstick after I was finished with the rice and beans. They said I had to learn my lesson, but never clued me in on which in particular I should concentrate.

Back when I could breathe easy and remain upright I kicked it around from place to place, doing odd jobs for whomever was kind enough to hire me.

I'd spend my money on liquor and women and the odd double feature. Sometimes I'd pay for one movie but wind up spending a whole day and night in the theater.

I never did learn a trade, and for that I'm regretful.

But still I drew a paycheck or loved a woman in almost all the fifty states except the ones in the lower lefthand corner. I never bought what everyone tried to sell as dry heat, though maybe that would've been best for my damaged lungs.

There was one woman that proved I was a slowdown on the uptake and something was bad wrong like my father said.

I was in a saloon minding my own and what was left of a whiskey sour. On the jukebox was an old favorite, Milk Cow Blues by Blind Manny Martinez. He was going on about how that sun looked good going down and everything was fine until a cross-eyed complication with bright blue eye shadow sat down next to me and started talking out loud in math problems. She said things like, suppose that R is closed under multiplication.

I told her I'm not one to hazard guesses, that I was no good with supposition or supplication, whichever it was.

She said it was fractal geometry and that I should keep quiet when she was speaking. Then she withdrew a bar napkin from its canister and marked it up. The R was lowercase and looked like a gun. She said she'd been working on this problem for years. She asked me what was wrong, why I was coughing. She said I was handsome.

The trouble is I'm human like most people and sometimes I have human needs. The ones that keep you up at night and have you reaching between your legs.

She had a leather handbag wrapped round her body that bisected her breasts. She reached in and retrieved graph paper and an abacus, said her father was a scientist.

She had a way of rubbing my back as I was coughing, and by the time I came to she was gone along with my wallet and jewelry.

This happened only a few times, and when I asked her about it she said I was confused, that it wasn't her and I couldn't prove anything.

We never talked about ourselves in relation to other people except once or twice. She talked about her son who always called her at work and would get her in trouble.

I always tried to afford her the benefit of whatever doubt I could muster.

After a while she stopped coming to the saloon and I didn't know whatever became of her.

Here in Luck, though, none of this amounts to anything. You make the mistake of getting born and then you're surrounded by people who take liberties and then this happens and that and you wind up on the ground hungry and cold with only a knapsack to lay your head upon.

Sometimes people come by and feign concern. They feed me soup, and I tell them about Manny and his theories and what water does to wood. I tell them about the emphysema. I never tell them about my parents and the back room or the woman who robbed me all the time.

Sometimes they ask me to come home with them, but I almost always refuse.

Only once did I go home with someone after an invitation.

The woman wore a pleated skirt that billowed in the wind so I figured it was safe. She said she had just been run over by a bicycle and could use the company. Her hand was bandaged and there was blood on her peasant blouse.

She offered me a drink and sat me down on a leather couch that had duct tape keeping it together. She asked me for a foot massage but I told her I couldn't, that my hands were no good on account of the syndrome. She said she was disappointed in me, and I told her I was disappointed, too.

She spoke of matters great and small. I lost track of the conversation when she bemoaned the polar ice caps and how they were melting. She spoke of starving polar bears and ravenous corporations. Right around this time a bee buzzed past her face and she spent the rest of the evening trying to kill it.

This is when I excused myself and left her alone forever.

All I want is to sleep through the night and listen to the rain.

Only sometimes do I think about that woman in Wyoming or Ohio or wherever it was.

When I forget myself and let the woman and her son slip into conversation it makes everyone uncomfortable.

It has the same effect on me because I'm no different, not by any measure.

The Office and Affairs of Love

Don't wake up this morning, don't look out the door.

Silence Is the Perfectest Herald of Joy

I unfold and place the napkin on my lap. It likely won't stay there. I always place the napkin on my lap and it always falls to the floor before I am finished. I am unaware of this when it happens. What I mean is I always reach for the napkin in my lap at the end of the meal and it is never there.

I sometimes look around to see if anyone is watching, but no one is ever watching. It is as if I am not a corporeal being and this is why I never pick up the napkin once it has fallen.

But I am indeed a corporeal being trying to eat my lunch in peace and all I want is to finish quietly and then everyone can go off and have a good day.

This includes Esperanza, my puzzle and punishment.

Once I asked Esperanza what do you have tomorrow. She answered, my dignity.

I wanted to meet with her, to discuss the future. She didn't want this. She didn't want to meet and she didn't want a future.

Tomorrow I will turn her in.

I am without choice.

The waitress brings me a turkey club, which is what I ordered. This waitress doesn't always bring what I've ordered. Once she brought me a Reuben when I'd ordered French toast. I asked what is the meaning of this and she didn't know what to say. She stood there and looked scared or pathetic. I sometimes can't tell the difference, how people look.

The waitress wants my children. Every other woman I meet wants to have my children. It's exhausting.

Esperanza is the lone glorious exception. She wants nothing at all from me and has said this to me repeatedly. She says, I want nothing at all from you.

There is almost no room for misinterpretation.

Esperanza and all the waitresses here are illegal because they are aliens. They hail from a godforsaken place that a band of hooligans invaded and then one thing and another for hundreds of years.

She and the others are products of this atrocity.

I have to turn them in because I always do what's right.

They call me the beacon of virtue and justice and when I say they I mean hardly anyone.

Also, I have to turn them in before they turn me in.

They bring me food like this to rile me, have been doing it since I started coming here.

My brother Manny is the one who told me about this place. He wishes me dead and curses me every time I see him, but otherwise is a fine fellow.

What to say about my brother that hasn't been said countless times already.

He is a man like everyone else, like millions of others. He is weak. He is pitiful. He will live a tedious everyday life bringing happiness or joy to no one and then die prematurely at an inconvenient time.

Our mother always favored him which proves something about everybody.

I am almost always bored. This is what happens when you want nothing, when you were born about ten thousand years ago and have lived too many lives and in this most recent incarnation you are finally without ambition.

My mother would ask, what do you want to do today? I would answer, nothing. She would say, don't you want to go to the park, play with your brother and his friends? I would say, no. I would say, I don't like the park and I don't like my brother and his friends.

Once I visited someone who called herself a healer. She had me remove my clothes and lie down on a massage table. She lit candles, burned incense, played sitar music. She moved her hands all over my body and then above it. She made motions like she was pulling something out of me, some kind of rope or my intestines. I believe I was being spiritually disemboweled. I refrained from comment or question.

She said I'd been strangled in a past life. I told her that wasn't the half of it.

At night I dream lives though not my own.

These are the remnants, the debris of past incarnations. I can almost recognize the people and places.

I have walked the earth on every continent, too many times.

I have been known to sleep for up to sixteen hours at a chance. Once I am finished sleeping I don't want to eat breakfast as I am never hungry after waking.

I never want to leave the house or stay home. I don't want to watch television or listen to music or read a book.

They all look like peasants, like natives of an exotic land, the women who want my children, but I won't give them the satisfaction and I won't do that to an innocent unborn.

All the time between lives I fight to stay unborn but then someone somewhere foists life upon me yet again.

This is what life is like in the astral plane. It's a bullfight in zero gravity.

I haven't fathered or mothered a child myself in hundreds of years.

These women who want and hate me all have the dark hair and complexion and that feminine curvature no one thinks is a good idea.

This also describes Esperanza, who haunts me. I must've been someone awful in the most recent life, someone worse than my brother.

Esperanza is the only thing I've ever wanted which proves desire is good for nothing.

I try to eat the turkey club, but I fail.

I wish I were dead or could stop being born.

Once I was hanged from a poplar tree. Once I was run through in front of my family. Another time I was set adrift on an ice floe at the age of one hundred and four.

I need this turkey club to be the highlight of my day, a reason for living. There is nothing I have to do later or want to do and my leg hurts.

This is how I woke up this morning. I took one step out of bed and noticed that my leg hurt. I had to hobble to the bathroom so I could shower and the hot water could massage my leg.

Our parents both disappeared, but not at the same time. They had my brother first and realized it was a mistake that could only be corrected by me. This is when they realized that I was also a mistake and there could be no corrective measures after that.

My father left first, on a Monday when I was five years old. This is what I've been told, as I have no memory of this happening. My mother told me there were two reasons my father left and my brother and I were both of them.

Then my mother left that Friday and they sent us to live with a series of aunts and uncles.

I could order something else, send back this turkey club and berate them ceaselessly. I could call the authorities and have everyone deported.

I could do almost anything.

I could read a book but who cares.

I could see a movie but who cares.

I could call a friend but I don't think I have any. I'm not sure what makes a friend a friend or if the people I know qualify as such. I don't enjoy seeing or talking to them and I'm sure they feel likewise.

Sister in the Basement, Manny Elsewhere

Sister is in the basement washing dishes with cold water. It takes forever for the water to run hot and sometimes it never does. Sister isn't practiced in patience or foresight, has no truck with anything involving the future or time. She can't see Monday sitting atop Sunday night's shoulders.

Once she waited fifteen minutes for the water to run hot and decided never again.

Manny is elsewhere, maybe at work or on the train ride home.

Sister is in the basement after a day of sublime indifference to the world. She never left the confines of her makeshift bedroom, didn't pick up a book or magazine, didn't turn on a television or radio. Her cellphone didn't ring or vibrate and she never once looked at it. She didn't look at a clock, either, because there isn't one anywhere in the basement. She stayed in bed the whole day, shifted from back to side to stomach and slept and dozed and drifted in and out of dreams both pleasant and unnerving and when she finally got herself upright she thought about how much she enjoyed sleeping and resolved to do as much as she possibly could in the coming days, weeks, months.

Meanwhile, Manny was at work or in a hospital bed hooked up to an IV drip or downtown at a peep show or tangled up with one of his colleagues in a broom closet or motel room, a woman named Sofia or Esperanza or a man named Bill or Sharon.

Sister doesn't care any which way.

Look at Sister there in the basement, doing dishes with cold water and looking forward to bedtime, working her way to the bottom of a too-crowded sink.

What Doesn't Help Me Sleep

IF YOU SURVIVE CHILDHOOD do not continue your schooling or get a job or start a family or participate in society. Instead run away to the mountains and never be heard from again. Commune only with nature if nature hasn't already done away with you.

Essential Living

If you survive nature maybe write a book about it. Talk about plants and animals and bodies of water. Talk about your beans and chairs and how you leave one for society should society drop by unannounced. If you finish the book go back to the beginning and consider how you went wrong at every turn. Change every word to its opposite so that night becomes day and young becomes old and life becomes death and then remove all punctuation. When you are finished for the second time take the manuscript to the nearest body of water and fashion each page into a model boat. Once you have enough for a flotilla or armada, sit back and watch each page sail away. When the last vessel is out of sight, collect the remainder of your firewood and place each log carefully into the hearth. If you are still dressed, remove each item of clothing to feel the warmth of the fire on your bare skin.

Too Long Life

THERE ARE PEOPLE who believe they have lived before. These people speak of past lives and how they were once a prospector, a tanner, a despotic ruler. They say they were born ten thousand years ago and they can't stop being born. They say they've been men and women, rich and poor, black and white and brown. They have killed other people and been killed by other people. At night they stay awake and listen to the rain, which sounds today the way it sounded thousands of years ago when they were a slave, when they were the shaman of a nomadic tribe, when they were a troubadour playing lilting ballads and haunting dirges for anyone who would listen.

Tarry Not Long Gentle Courtesan

I HAVE A NOISE MACHINE set to falling rain and it helps me sleep. I'm not sure why falling rain helps me sleep because most nights I stay up for hours and listen to the falling rain instead of falling asleep like I'm supposed to do. This is exactly how it was in the shed growing up. Sometimes I'd stay up the whole night waiting for the rain to stop because only then was it safe to sleep or maybe it was the other way around. That it was only safe to fall asleep once it started raining because my parents wouldn't come out to beat me. My parents didn't like the rain and wouldn't come out to the shed until it stopped. Once I was out there alone for a whole week during a deluge that flooded most of the town.

The only time I remember my parents in the rain was the night I saw a little girl who might've been my sister hiding behind them as they walked out to the shed. The reason I think she might've been my sister is she looked exactly like me only with hair and shorter. I asked them who is that standing behind you and they answered by kicking me repeatedly because they'd left the nightstick in the house. I didn't ask about the little girl after that and I don't know whatever became of her. Now I rarely stay up the whole night so the sound machine works more often than otherwise. Even so I can't decide if I like the sound of falling rain from the noise machine better than the sound of falling rain from the sky. I try to compare the two sounds and I listen for patterns in clusters of rain or the differences between the collision of water and dirt as opposed to wood or tin or any material they use to construct a roof, but I know the sky is no longer up in the sky, which is why I prefer the noise machine now.

A Mother Like This One

THERE IS PROBABLY an office building, a compact car, a woman who works for a modest living. She is probably an honest woman, so let's not assume anything about her because she is left-handed and cross-eyed. That she wears blue eye shadow shouldn't bother us, either. This is how she was raised, so we can forgive her more than this. If she has a family she is probably good to them. She might even wake early to cook them breakfast, usually scrambled eggs, though sometimes it's waffles. If she has a son it's probably the son who begs her to make them every morning, guilts her into it about twice a week, although there's never time for this. This is what she says to him, she says, I don't have time for this. She is always late to work whenever she makes waffles for her son, if she has a son, which she probably does. The creases in her forehead and the way she carries her oversized brown leather handbag across her body, bisecting her breasts, tell us she has a son, one who likes waffles a little too much. After the waffles she drives her compact car to work, probably to a restaurant where she is a waitress, otherwise it's an office building as an administrative assistant or CEO. The building is not a high-rise, doesn't have complicated architecture, it's a building like so many others, utilitarian, nondescript. Let us give her the benefit of whatever doubt we can muster.

Once at work behind her desk, inside her cubicle, she receives phone calls from her son, roughly once an hour. What they talk about is between the two of them and not our concern. We won't even speculate as to the nature of their conversations. What's more important is that her bosses understand or rather they tell her they understand, but the truth is they don't like it. They don't like it any more than we do. They tell her as long as it doesn't take away from her duties and she tells them her son is special, but it's not true. There is nothing special about her son, if she does indeed have one. After all, this woman has lied before. She even lied to get this job, telling the bosses during her interview that she had five years of administrative experience, that she helped run her father's business before he died. Her father was a police officer, has never once owned a business, and is still living, though he has been ill and will finally succumb to cirrhosis of the liver in six months, dying alone in his shower after not feeling up to his daily walk in the park. The woman will ask her neighbor, Esperanza, to watch her son for a few days while she tends to her father's affairs. She tells Esperanza that her father drank away her inheritance, so she won't be returning with any money and won't be able to pay her. She says her life is an unrelenting tragedy with no reprieve. She says she can't even afford to feed herself sometimes, especially when her boss can't make payroll. There's no telling if this is true. Suppose this woman skips lunch three times a week. We can't be sure if she's being thrifty or trying to lose weight or lying. Sometimes she cries poverty and sometimes she wonders if the reason she is still single is due to her figure, as she has put on perhaps twenty pounds in the past year or two. She once described herself as model-thin to attract a date so this is the kind of duplicity we're talking about here. The woman is shapely, what some might characterize as voluptuous or buxom. We wouldn't put it past her to fabricate a son.

Don't let the leg-warmers and canvas sneakers fool you, this woman is clever. If her son is real, if he actually exists, doubtless he is inappropriately affectionate with her. He is always hugging her a little too closely; kissing her forehead, her neck. At night he crawls into bed next to her and they wake up together the next morning. They even have their own special language. No one can understand what they say to each other, but it sounds like baby talk, like gibberish. This makes everyone uncomfortable and we're no different. We don't like to see this sort of thing because we've seen it before and we know what it means.

What They Won't Tell You in School

If you make the mistake of securing employment do not show up to work early or stay late. Do not do more than what is required. Do not eat lunch with colleagues or meet them for drinks after work. Do not order a martini up with a twist at happy hour or bat cleanup on the company softball team. Do not join anyone for dinner or attend a holiday party. Always tell people you have other plans and you're very sorry but you want for everybody to have a wonderful time.

What's Not on the Radio

THE SONG ISN'T ON THE RADIO because there is no song, the same as there is no radio. If there were a song it would be a slow blues or shuffle, probably in E major, probably called Milk Cow Blues. There would be no person in the song as subject or object, no milk or cow mentioned in the lyrics, just as there would be no one playing the song and no one singing the song. Perhaps there would be the memory of a song, something like a faint echo barely audible, but there will be no one to remember or hear it.

Ready for to Fade

MANNY WAS BLEEDING and would probably be dead in an hour or two. Still, I couldn't get Esperanza off me. I said to Esperanza, listen, Manny is bleeding and will probably dead in an hour or two. Esperanza said, doesn't that get you going? I said, we probably shouldn't do this anymore. Then Esperanza said, I'll have your baby. I know your wife won't do that. Meanwhile, Manny was bleeding and would probably be dead in an hour or two. I said to Esperanza, maybe one of us should go for help. Esperanza said, I'll never see you again. She said, how can you do this. She said, you don't even like Manny. It was true, I didn't like Manny and never did. This is when Esperanza started taking off her clothes. First it was the top, which was sheer or see-through, which made it possible to see her tattoo, which she called an ambigram, it read *I'm fine* or *Save Me* depending on how you looked at it, and then it was the skirt, which I always thought she looked great in. It was long and pleated and she would make it twirl whenever she danced. Once she tried to teach me the shim-sham but I didn't like how mechanical it was, this foot up and back then the opposite followed by the other and it was too much to concentrate on. Still, I liked watching Esperanza do it, and so did Manny. This is why I started laughing and kept on laughing until Esperanza was naked.

Somewhere I knew Sister was doing dishes in cold water and Sofia was tormenting a troupe of suitors. I thought about other people I've known and wondered how they might feel when they hear about Manny. By this time, it was almost six in the morning and a new day was starting outside the kitchen window. I could see a sliver of the everywhere sky, which looked closer to the ground than it should, and the clouds that appeared to be a descending army in white tanks. I watched a family of blackbirds flitting between the trees like they didn't know what to do with themselves, like it was a free-for-all. I looked at Esperanza, incandescent in the yellow morning light, and Esperanza looked at me and there were no sounds coming from outside, not even the birds chirping at each other.

There Was a Star Danced and Under That Were You Born

RIGHT AWAY you think cancer.

No Ocean, Nor Water

THERE'S NEITHER OCEAN NOR WAVES to move the ocean to east from west or north from south. There's no water in lakes or ponds or rivers or brooks. There are no canals or channels or creeks, no estuaries, no gulfs, no inlets, no lagoons, no marshes, no pools, no puddles, no reservoirs, no streams or straits or springs.

Say No More

A LOT OF PEOPLE say I have great posture. I'm not sure this is true, but I hear it from people all the time, including the woman cleaning my kitchen. She has been here for two hours and thus far she has finished cleaning the bathroom and is in the process of cleaning the kitchen. She is slated to be here for another hour as I paid upfront for three. I have remained in the living room while she has been cleaning, as I do not want to make her uncomfortable or feel as though I'm scrutinizing her work. I'm sometimes accused of making people uncomfortable but I don't think this is my fault. I can't help how I look or that I am not good with small talk or casual conversation. But finally I had to use the bathroom and had no choice. I apologized for disturbing her as I walked through the kitchen, said I would only be a moment, opened and closed the bathroom door as quietly as possible. I did this about thirty minutes ago and it seemed she wasn't bothered. She continued what she was doing, cleaning the stove I believe, and didn't acknowledge me. I noticed, too, that she wasn't naked. I'm not saying that she is supposed to be naked, that I've paid for a naked cleaning service, because it isn't true. I paid for a traditional cleaning service, one that I've used now several times. Some people might call me a fanatic about cleanliness, but my question is what's wrong with that. I spend a decent amount of time cleaning the apartment myself but I also need an expert to come in every couple of weeks. I wasn't expecting her to be naked when I walked through the kitchen to get to the bathroom. I've heard that people like to clean naked so as not to soil their clothes or garner a bigger tip. Nothing like this was discussed when she arrived at eleven this morning and I can't remember where I heard these stories or if it was my mother or father or sister who told me. Sometimes my sister would tell me certain things and I'd have to tell her to stop because I didn't want to hear it. She'd go on about her private sexual affairs, for instance, what she'd like to do to people or have done to her. It could be my sister was a naked maid herself, may've even offered to clean my apartment that way. This is when I told her I didn't want to hear it, so it doesn't matter what I disclose or whose confidence I'm breaking.

When it comes to naked housecleaning, it could be something I saw on television or overheard in a bar or restaurant. I don't generally go to bars or restaurants so this seems unlikely. I can't abide any sort of noise, either from people or machines, which is why I don't go to bars or restaurants. I can't even listen to music anymore. If someone says hello to me I ask them to write me a letter instead. The only thing the woman who is cleaning my kitchen said to me upon arrival was that I had great posture, which I'm not sure is true. What I mean to say is I'm not sure I have great posture and I'm not sure that's what she said. The woman who is cleaning my kitchen doesn't speak English and my Polish or German or Russian is rusty. I used to be able to speak Polish and German in other lifetimes, but when you don't practice for hundreds of years you forget almost everything. I think this is where she is from, the woman who is cleaning my kitchen with all of her clothes on, as she looks as though she is from that part of the world. She is tall and thin with prominent cheekbones. She has blonde hair and lifeless blue eyes, which describes most of her compatriots. She herself has great posture and is standing perfectly upright when she isn't bending over to clean in hard-to-reach corners. She and I have only made eye contact two or three times, as we are both shy people. I can't speak for her, but I was born shy and have been shy my whole life. I almost never speak unless I am spoken to and not always then. Nine out of ten people shunned by their parents and who were made to live in a shed out in the backyard aren't what one might call well-adjusted.

People are sometimes mystified by my silence; they think I'm uncaring or aloof. I'm not sure this is true, but I'm often baffled by people and am rendered dumb in their presence. This is why I always prefer staying home. I'm certain the woman who is cleaning the kitchen is the same way. I could tell by the way she never looks up when I make a noise or how when I told her my name she said nothing in return. Perhaps she is only shy when she works or because English isn't her native language. Perhaps when she is out with her friends in Minsk she is bold and aggressive, the sort of woman who gets up on tabletops and dances to pop songs in her underwear. I rarely wear underwear myself, as I find it too constricting. In fact, I was naked before she arrived to clean my apartment. I am often naked in my apartment, as I can rarely muster the effort of dressing myself in the morning. Normally I have to eat a full breakfast before I can manage getting dressed, which I only do if I have an appointment. Breakfast can consist of nonfat yogurt and store-bought granola, but rarely includes berries or bananas or fruit of any kind. I never eat cereal for breakfast, either, not the oat cereal I enjoyed as a child or the muesli I used to eat years ago. Only sometimes will I scramble or fry two or three eggs depending on my appetite, but I've never poached or boiled an egg in my life. Sometimes I separate and then dispose of the yolks in an effort to lower cholesterol. I'm not sure if I should limit my cholesterol intake, but both my father and grandfather died young of heart attacks. I'm also not sure if yolks increase your cholesterol and I'm not sure I care anymore. Whenever I do make eggs, which is infrequent at best, I'll slide two pieces of whole wheat or multigrain bread into the toaster, which I'll dress with Irish butter, but never any jelly or jam or marmalade or preserves. Only once or twice a year will I prepare steel-cut oats for breakfast. Normally I will not measure out how much water is needed according to the ratio on the can. The recommended serving for one is insubstantial and I can never figure out how much more to make. I refuse to stand over the stove to stir oatmeal every two or so minutes for half an hour is my problem, and then it gets burned. I've never used a blender to make breakfast, which I understand some people do. They call it a smoothie and they put almost anything in it. This doesn't seem right to me, not the process, nor the ridiculous word they call it. I never drink anything when I eat breakfast except for water. I can't drink coffee for the caffeine and what it does to my bladder and sleep patterns and I can't drink orange juice for the same reasons. Once in a while I'll make an herbal tea as I enjoy the taste. Drinking tea makes me feel like I'm at home even though I almost never feel that way.

I've never in my life made French toast or pancakes or waffles for the effort involved, which is beyond my meager capabilities. I have a memory of my mother making me waffles one morning, but I'm not sure this actually happened. Sometimes I can't distinguish between what's real and what I've dreamed or saw in a movie when it comes to my own life story. It's also possible that I'm referring to a past life. This is why one experiences déjà vu, and for me it's always about breakfast. But I only eat breakfast if I have to leave the apartment and I only leave the apartment if I have an appointment. Sometimes I have to visit a doctor or dentist or accountant. There is something wrong with my hearing and something wrong with my gums and something wrong with my finances. Getting dressed includes wearing earplugs, which I do whenever I leave the house. Sometimes I have to wear earplugs inside the house because the downstairs neighbor plays dance music at earsplitting volumes. This is when I imagine committing certain violent acts which always conclude with arson, but I never have any matches so I never go through with it. I've tried talking with the downstairs neighbor, but it's pointless as he is a cretin who won't listen to reason. Sometimes I leave the house instead of murdering him and then burning down the building and sometimes I wear headphones, too, as extra protection from all that noise. I can't hear anything when I'm wearing both earplugs and headphones at the same time. I'm sure one day I'll be totally deaf, if I live long enough, so in this way it's like practice. Both my mother and grandmother went deaf, but neither was ever so sensitive to noise that they had to wear earplugs and headphones whenever they went outside. Perhaps this is why they went deaf in the first place. It's possible I might be saving what little hearing I have left with these prophylactic measures. If I'm ever run over by a bus or truck, it will be when I am wearing earplugs and headphones at the same time. I've almost been run over several times already. The problem is I never pay attention when I am out on the streets and I cross against the lights. One time someone had to pull me out of the way of an oncoming eighteen-wheeler. It was quite a sensation—being jerked back by the shirt collar and feeling the whoosh of air as the truck sped past. I couldn't hear myself thank the person who saved my life, but I'm pretty sure I did thank him. If he said something in reply I couldn't hear that, either, as the headphones were still securely on my head. I remember watching a movie where a woman was run over by a city bus and died in a stranger's arms. I remember wondering what it must feel like to lie on the ground after you've been mortally wounded, what you might look at and think about in that moment. Perhaps you'd look up into the sky and find a cloud that resembles a president or Jesus. I've never seen a cloud that looked like anything but I've heard stories about others who do. Maybe you'd listen to the wind and find a kind of music in that sound. I never listen to music when I'm wearing the headphones, as that would defeat the purpose.

The last woman who came over to clean did so with headphones on the entire time. I do not know what she was listening to and I didn't ask. This woman wasn't Polish or Czech, but rather from somewhere in Central America. Someplace awful where the weather is unbearable and there are monkeys and bugs and hundreds of years ago marauding Europeans discovered it and turned everyone Catholic after raping and pillaging them first. I was born Catholic, was baptized as an infant and received First Communion as a child and then got confirmed as a teenager. After that I never went back to church, as I found the entire practice tedious and futile. Both my deaf mother and grandmother were zealots, though perhaps that is too strong a term. A zealot is fanatical and neither my mother nor grandmother could be described this way. It's true they visited church often and spent hours every day saying novenas, but they never proselytized or served God in a profound manner. They were devout, in fact my mother still is. She is almost one hundred years old and manages to go to church several times a week. I can't remember exactly when she disowned me as it was a long time ago. The whys and wherefores don't matter anymore, but I'm sure my lack of faith played a part in it. I seem to remember her using the word heretic. I'm not sure if she disowned my brother at the same time or subsequent to my disownment. I don't harbor ill will toward any of them, not my mother or brother or the woman who got hit by the city bus and looked up to see Jesus in the clouds. I also don't harbor ill will toward the cleaning woman, though I still believe she stole from me. I can't prove this but I also can't find the antique flask I'd had for over thirty years.

The flask was a gift from a friend for standing up at his wedding. It's the only wedding I've ever attended and the only time I've worn a tuxedo. I was a member of his wedding party, a groomsman, though I had no official responsibilities. In fact, I can't recall the event at all, except to say that I might be lying. I can recall the rehearsal dinner the night before the wedding, but not the wedding ceremony or reception. There wasn't a rehearsal during the rehearsal dinner. Nobody recited lines, stood in assigned places, hit marks. There was a dinner at a restaurant and everyone around the table said something, including the bride and groom. What I remember is that the bride toasted her mother, babbled until she said her mother was a diamond in the rough. There was a moment of silence or nervous laughter and then the bride's future mother-in-law corrected her, said I'm pretty sure your mother is finished. Then there was more nervous laughter and silence and this is when I hoped a city bus was on the way to run us over.

I'm not sure what the bride meant or what she intended to say. For years I tried to figure this out. I can't remember what I said that night, though I believe I said something. I might've recited a poem, something like, *within me tis as if the green and climbing eyesight of a cat has crawled near my mind's poor birds*. I'm sure everyone looked at me askance, like there was something wrong with me. Now I don't talk unless it's necessary and I try not to recite poetry in front of people. Not a sonnet, not a villanelle, not even a limerick. The groom was an old friend, someone I went to school with and knew for twenty years. I couldn't keep up with him any longer due to his political affiliations, which were heinous, but the disillusion happened years later. Still, I treasured the flask and was shocked and disappointed to find it gone.

This particular cleaning woman, the one who I'm certain stole it, wasn't tall or thin, but rather short and corpulent. She wore a gold crucifix around her neck and remained clothed while cleaning my apartment. She said her name was Sofia or Esperanza. It's possible I've had two cleaning ladies and I'm conflating the two. Regardless, I contacted the agency and filed a complaint, but I couldn't prove anything and the cleaning woman denied any wrongdoing. I never suggested she should get deported and realized this might happen were I to press the matter. This is when I reversed course and told the agency I found the flask and withdrew my complaint. I even wrote the cleaning woman a glowing review, though I still believe she's a thief. I don't regret not turning her in as I only turn people in if they are illegal aliens. The thought has occurred to me that if she were naked she'd have nowhere to hide contraband, which is perhaps one virtue of hiring a naked maid. I'm not sure why anyone chooses to wear clothes when not absolutely necessary. In my own apartment I never bother getting dressed, as there is no one here to see me, except for maybe the people in the park across the street. I'm not sure if anyone in the park has seen me naked, but I sometimes leave the blinds open and I am always naked in here. The only living things that see me naked are the plants. A few months ago, I bought some houseplants and a tree, and they need sunlight to stay alive. I'm always mindful of this even though I don't care for the sun or its light. I come from a long line of fair-skinned people, though hereditarily we should all be swarthy, as I descend from peoples near the Mediterranean and Caribbean seas. Several family members have contracted all manner of skin-related catastrophes, from sunspots to terminal melanoma. In fact, before I bought the plants I never had the blinds open, not even once. I have blackout curtains hanging in the living room where the plants are, so when I said blinds I was mistaken. I'm not sure why I said blinds when I meant curtains. I know the difference between the two, as I have blinds in the bathroom. The blinds were hanging in the bathroom when I moved in. However, I did go out and purchase the blackout curtains and hung them over the bay windows in the living room. I felt accomplished that day because I'm useless more often than otherwise.

Almost no light filters through the blackout curtains, so I have to pull them back for the plants. I'm also careful to water the plants once a week, which is what the clerk at the nursery told me to do. One of the plants seems to require more water than the others. The leaves sag if it goes too long without water. It's almost funny, the sight of these drooping leaves, but I never laugh because I will feel awful if the plant dies before I do. I'm almost like a parent, which I never could be in real life. There are too many people in the world and it would be best if my genes die with me. Another reason I don't have children is I don't want to run into them during my next life. This has happened more than once and it's always disappointing to see how they turned out. I do like the plants, however, and don't know why it's never occurred to me to buy plants before. I have no imagination is the problem. I can survive on bread and water and a comfortable bed, as long as there is air conditioning. I probably couldn't live without air conditioning. It feels like I'm going to choke and die when it's too hot, when I'm sweating and can't stop. I sweat all the time in the summer, even in bed when I have the air conditioner on. It is no way to go through life, but go through it I do, every day without fail. For what purpose and to what end I've no idea, though I suppose it's the same one that ends everybody. All that's left is the when and how and the answers are probably soon and unspeakable.

Sometimes I wonder if I should commit suicide instead of waiting, but I don't know how I would do it or what would inflict the least amount of pain. I'm sure someone somewhere has shot himself to see what it feels like. The world is this sort of place. I remember a young colleague once telling me a story of how he and his friends waterboarded each other. I've had no such desire, though I have imagined pouring boiling water over my head and genitals or stepping in front of a moving train or truck. I've imagined all sorts of things, but executing is another matter. This morning, I wondered what would happen if, when the maid arrived, I'd answered the door naked. I wondered if she would recoil in fear and horror or if she would be nonchalant. There is nothing inherently threatening about a naked man. You can probably say a naked man is less threatening than his clothed counterpart as you know exactly what you're dealing with, there can be no weapons concealed anywhere. I know that I mean no harm to anyone but who would know that by looking. Still, I could never do such a thing as I am as much a slave to convention and courtesy as anyone. The only thing I couldn't do to make a guest comfortable in my own home is turn off the air conditioner. I keep a closet full of sweaters and coats in case someone gets cold. But I am careful to move the plants away from the air conditioner, as I'm sure it's not good for them. No one told me this, but there are certain things one knows without being told. I'm not sure how long plants are supposed to live and I'm not sure how long I'm supposed to live, either. If I were to go to a doctor for something other than my hearing I'm certain I'd be told I have only months. The reason I believe this is I wake in the middle of the night gasping for air more than what's normal. I am always sweating when I wake up like this. I think I stop breathing but something jolts me awake before I can drift off into whatever comes next.

I've been alive for almost fifty years and it's never occurred to me to buy a houseplant or go to a nursery. I may've mentioned that already. I find I repeat myself more as I get older. People say, you already told me this, and I curse myself for lending voice to thought in the first place. You can't repeat yourself if you remain mute. Not too long ago I had a friend visiting from out of town, and she suggested I buy plants to give the apartment life and color, and I didn't respond so that I wouldn't repeat myself. This is the friend who I once shared a hotel room with for three days and nights but nothing ever happened. We were attending a conference and figured we could reduce expenses by sharing a room even though there was only one bed. One night after drinking too much, she curled into me and said, there's a fog. She pushed her lips into mine and I put my arms around her body, moving my hands over her back down to the top of her buttocks. She said, there's a fog, and then she said, if you want to stick it in me you can but we won't be friends anymore. I didn't know what to do or say so I didn't do or say anything. I thought about how for years I wanted to see my friend naked or have her see me naked and how that might lead to sexual communication. I thought about what I should hide from the cleaning lady for the next appointment and then I thought about fog and the weather conditions that create fog. After all this thought I didn't stick anything anywhere and a few minutes later she was asleep and so we are still friends to this day. This is how I could have her over for a visit even though I'm sure we could still visit together if I did stick it in her like she offered. I'm not sure sticking it in automatically nullifies a friendship of ten years, but it's hard to know these kinds of things. She said she was jealous of the natural light I have because where she lives there's none. This is when I told my friend that if something happens in the middle of the night then she has to come to my apartment to water the plants. I told her she can live here if she wants to, but she should know the cleaning lady might steal her things and the downstairs neighbor might play loud dance music at all hours and you might one day want to murder him and then set the building on fire. I told her if that's okay with you then the plants will be your responsibility.

Esperanza Once

Esperanza once thought about changing her name.

Esperanza Once

ESPERANZA ONCE SAID, I do have memories, but I never indulge in them. I keep most of them in a strong box in the basement of a rented house in a far-off country somewhere else. She said they are not misty or water-colored or pressed between any pages in my mind. Once in a great while they are stories to tell at parties to make it seem as though I've lived a real life.

When the Noise Machine Doesn't Work

The noise machine makes other noises but they never induce sleep for me so I never listen to them. One is the sound of the ocean slamming against the shore and another is a thunderstorm, which has never relaxed me in any way. How anyone can find a thunderclap soothing mystifies me. The ocean has always made me nervous, as I'm sure I'd drown were I to find myself on top of or inside it. I can't swim anymore is the reason, but I think I could when I was a child. I have memories of swimming in a pool, of taking lessons, but maybe this happened to me in a dream or I saw it in a movie or I could swim in a previous life. This kind of confusion was how it felt when I almost drowned. It was Esperanza who saved me. We were on someone's boat for a party and we crashed into a lighthouse and capsized. All of us went into the water but I was the only one who couldn't swim. I remember getting sucked under by the current, swallowing a lungful of dirty river water. I remember being disoriented and losing consciousness and floating in the water and it reminded me of the astral plane between worlds. This is when Esperanza rushed over to drag me to the rocks surrounding the lighthouse. She asked if I was okay and I answered by hyperventilating for a minute or two. She shook her head at me like I'd done something wrong. That is my tragedy, if I have one, which I do and her name is Esperanza. Regardless, I don't think about this when I'm trying to sleep, which is why I don't have the noise machine set to the pounding surf because who wants to think of Esperanza anymore.

No Greater Devotion

If you make the mistake of leaving your house, turn around and go back inside. Make sure the doors are locked and the windows are shut. Draw the curtains and do not allow any sunlight to invade your home. Sunlight is not a disinfectant, so be sure to keep plenty of white vinegar on hand.

The Man and Woman Try to Have Sex

The man and woman have sex with each other about once or twice a month but would like to try more often. This is what they say to each other at night when they are too tired or unwell or distracted by the world to have sex.

They ask each other if something is wrong. One of them says, I'm not feeling well, I think it's something I ate, probably the meatless burrito. The other says, I didn't sleep last night, I have a headache, I think it's allergies or my new pillow. One of them says, it could be the dairy, I should try soymilk, and one of them says, we both should. The human body can't process dairy past childhood, one of them says. The other says, I think it's adolescence, but you're right. One of them says, my neck hurts, too, which can lead to headaches, but it could be high blood pressure. One of them says, maybe you should go to the doctor and the other one says, maybe we should lower our sodium intake and stop drinking and the other says maybe we should.

One of them says we should have more sex. The other agrees.

The man is middle aged. He can be tall or short, but is probably not thin. He is portly, but not rotund. He can be bald or have a full head of hair. If he has hair some of it is gray, but not all of it. He is not the sort for all of his hair to be gray. It is certainly not silver.

The woman is taller than the man and probably younger, but not much younger. She can rest her chin on the top of his head. She doesn't do this anymore, but years ago they'd perform this trick at parties. They called it a trick even though it is not a trick.

The average middle-aged couple has sex three times a day or five times per year depending on a variety of factors too confusing to delineate. This is according to a number of studies conducted by reputable agencies. The studies included couples of all genders and orientations, all races and ethnicities, all possible religious affiliations.

Neither the man nor woman is aware of the studies.

One of them says years ago and the other says it was different. One of them says are you mocking me and the other says I have to go to the drugstore, do you need anything?

The man and woman try to have sex but are interrupted for the laundry. The laundry knocks on the door and the man leaves the woman in the bedroom to go answer. His erection, which was still in the throes of forming, subsides on his way down the hall.

One of them says, what should we have for dinner? The other says, what are you in the mood for?

The man and woman met at a mutual friend's going-away party, a woman named Sofia.

This Sofia was going away soon, the next day, in the morning. It doesn't matter where Sofia was going. Sofia was going away from the man and woman and the place where they all lived. She had planned on returning, though, on picking up her life where she was hoping to leave it, maybe in a year or so.

It's possible both were in love with Sofia or had sexual fantasies involving her.

What the man and woman don't know about each other can fill volumes.

The woman asks the man about a past relationship. She asks if the woman was beautiful, if she was thin. She asks how long did you date her, did you ever consider cohabitation. She says, her name was Esperanza, right?

The man answers the questions and goes back to reading an article concerning the ongoing tragedy the federal government is ignoring and everyone is worried about.

The woman asks if the man has any questions for her, about her past relationships. She says, aren't you curious?

The man says he doesn't have any questions and he isn't curious. He says he lives in the moment and doesn't think about the past.

He says he dreams lives though not his own. He suspects he's lived countless lives, like that psychopathic general in World War II.

The woman asks if the man ever thinks about Esperanza or if he's been in touch with her. He says he doesn't think about her and hasn't been in touch with her for two years. The woman says, does this mean if we break up you won't think about me, either?

Years ago the man couldn't stop thinking about the former lovers of whomever he was having sex with at the time. He was haunted by the thoughts of bodies that violated or commingled with these women. Particularly the one who spoke of her libido exploding at the age of thirty and what she did as a result. One morning, entirely unprompted, she spoke of sex parties and swapping and the threesomes she'd had.

He couldn't stop seeing her mixed up in a tangle of bodies.

The man has only had one one-night stand in his life. It was with a woman named Lana or Layla. He remembers that she had curly hair, that she was in town from California. He remembers that he failed to orgasm and then he hailed a cab to take her back to her hotel in another borough of the city. The cabbie asked if Lana or Layla was his girlfriend and he said, she was tonight.

The woman has had several one-night stands, too many to count. Most of them occurred when she was traveling through Europe in her twenties. She once told the man she slutted her way through half the continent.

Neither the man nor the woman has any exotic fetishes.

The man has never considered having sex with an automobile, for instance, nor any other inanimate object. He has imagined having sex with many people, including friends and coworkers, strangers and acquaintances, aunts and cousins, cripples and dwarfs. He has imagined having sex with a woman who was once a man, but never the other way around. He thinks he might enjoy sex with a woman who was once a man. He is curious. He has never been curious about having sex with a man who was once a woman, nor has ever imagined having sex with a man at all, though it might depend upon what one considers sex. The man has imagined performing certain acts or having certain acts performed on him, but that is the entirety of what he has imagined.

He has heard about men having sex with animals but he has never imagined having sex with an animal. He doesn't think he'd be able to perform sex with an animal. Yet he doesn't pass judgment on those who have. He cannot imagine what it might be like to have a sheep, for instance, tempt one into sexual expression. He cannot imagine how long without human company one would have to go for a sheep to catch one's eye. Still, if he had to have sex with an animal, if someone put a gun to his head, he thinks he'd choose a dolphin. They seem clean and of good temperament.

The man and the woman don't try to have sex with each other in the living room. There they eat dinner and read a book or watch television or talk on the telephone with friends and family and don't have sex. Then they go to bed and don't have sex there. They fall asleep next to each other without either making a motion toward sex. In the middle of the night the man wonders if he should initiate sex but he's reluctant to interrupt the woman's sleep. The woman has had trouble sleeping lately, and it would be selfish of him to initiate sex because he is awake and can't sleep himself. Sometimes the man will put on the noise machine if he can't sleep and listen to the falling rain, but the woman doesn't like it. Sex would probably help the man fall asleep, and even though this is something the woman has consented to beforehand, as they'd discussed it several times and the woman said you can wake me up whenever you need to, she said the thought of it excites her, him waking her up for sex, putting moves on her while she is asleep, but even though the man said he would do it sometime he never does.

Earlier in the day they said let's have sex later, but now that it's later neither wants to.

The rest of the day passes without the mention of sex, without either one ever thinking about sex.

One of them says, do you think there's something wrong? The other says no, that it's normal. We're getting older and this is what happens.

He's wondered if he might want to try sex with someone else, if that might give him something of a jumpstart.

He hasn't thought of anyone specific except for Esperanza. He saw her dance one time at a party, her skirt twirling in the breeze around her, and that's what started everything.

The woman hasn't thought of having sex with someone else, or so she tells herself.

It's possible she's thought of having sex with any number of people, including Manny and Sister from down the street.

The man thinks someday he might say something out loud about opening the relationship, but he has no real desire to do so at this time.

The man thought he saw Esperanza on the street last week. This woman had the same hair and height and a similar gait. He considered trying to catch up to her, say hello, ask if she is proud of herself.

The man and woman have taken to watching porn as part of the foreplay ritual. Sometimes it's the only way either of them can spark a desire to have sex. The woman has never in her life watched porn, or so she tells the man.

The man, however, watches porn every other day, and years ago it was a daily practice. Now it's a habit that serves no function at all. Watching porn by himself fails to titillate him, and he wonders why he continues to do it.

The man asks the woman, what would you like to watch, and the woman asks the man, what do you like to watch? The man never answers because he is unsure as to how the woman might react. Instead, he takes her to the website he most often visits and shows her the homepage. They scan the various categories, which range from ridiculous to vile. The man studies the woman's face as she looks at the screen and is excited for the look in her eyes, a mix of curiosity, excitement, and repulsion.

The man and woman want to have sex with each other two or three times a week, but they both know this will never happen.

The man and woman resolve to act on such impulses when they arise. If one or the other wants to have sex they should make it clear. They should start in with a physical maneuver rather than say let's have sex later.

The man was involved with someone else before he met the woman. It was the mutual friend who was going away, and it was both tempestuous and confusing to the man.

The man isn't sure the woman knows about this, the entire uncensored history, even though everyone was friends with everyone else.

The man thinks something is wrong with him. Lately he has no libido at all. It's as if the production of testosterone or whatever is tied to energy and libido has been permanently suspended.

The man thinks it might be cancer or it could be that he's about to have a catastrophic cardiac event.

This has been going on for months now, maybe a year or two.

The man has seen too many movies where the man dies in the middle of sex, and while he knows full well the sex itself isn't what kills anyone, it becomes difficult not to think about.

The man thinks about dying while walking up a flight of stairs or shoveling snow, too.

He imagines what it might feel like and it's awful every time.

The man and woman have never once considered having sex outdoors. The man thinks it would be fun to try but hasn't brought it up.

The man likes the idea of being watched.

The man and woman don't have any children, and thus the children are never a reason they don't have sex.

The woman doesn't know the man thinks he might have cancer or die from a catastrophic cardiac event. She does know most of the man's relations have had cancer and none of those people look like they have sex with anyone.

The man thinks no one who has cancer ever has sex or ever wants to have sex.

The woman has fantasies about a group of men. The man doesn't mind this fantasy anymore, though years ago it would've killed him, like it did with the former lover whose libido exploded and she did things the man could only dream about.

The man says something about his libido, how it's not like it once was. The woman says, do you think something is wrong?

The man almost admits to what he's afraid of but decides against it. He remembers not feeling well for a year when he was younger, and the woman he was with then told him that she no longer viewed him in a sexual way. She said his inactivity was unappealing.

Maybe he did think he was dying once or twice during this time, but it never consumed him the way it does now because eventually he recovered from whatever was wrong with him and went about his life having sex with whomever was gracious enough to welcome him.

The man can't imagine ever feeling that sort of vitality again, and for this the man is bereft.

The man might finally see a doctor sometime next week. He might go for a full and thorough physical examination to try to determine what kind of cancer he might have or how much longer he can live before his heart explodes.

The man and woman try to have sex with each other and they try to have sex with each other and they try to have sex.

They are interrupted by almost anything. A sound in the hall, an earthquake in Mexico, a dance recital, an epidemic in Asia, the thought of a horrific death, either quick and sudden or slow and excruciating, a movie, a baseball game on television.

Sometimes saying out loud we should have sex or let's have sex later is the best they can do.

What's important is they are always sincere in their desire to have sex when they express such to each other, but then something happens or nothing happens or everything in the world happens and they don't have sex now and they don't have sex later and they never do. And maybe someday they never will again, but not now, not yet, not today.

Somehow Only We Got in Trouble

We didn't want Manny to die because most of us liked Manny and that tells you everything you need to know about the man. What we're saying is we enjoyed his company. We liked how he'd tell us jokes and eat his carrots and do his crossword puzzles. We always tried to help him with his crossword puzzles but he never wanted our help. He'd tell us to fuck off and what did we know. The truth is he was right, most of us didn't know anything. Once we tried to help him with a mountain in Asia and the natives who are expert mountaineers and he started crying and then someone said not this again and someone else started throwing punches and from there it was a free-for-all. Manny called it a donnybrook but we said it was more of a melee and then someone else called it a fracas and this is when everything went haywire. We probably all should have fucked off when we had the chance is the upshot. But Manny was always smarter than most of us or at least he seemed that way. It seemed like maybe he was older or climbed mountains himself or slept in the park. People who sleep in the park are always smart or talented like the painter with three French names. He'd show up every day with leaves in his hair and dirt under his nails, just like Jean-Michel Monet. We knew he'd be upset if someone asked him about the leaves in his hair or the dirt under his nails so we never did. This was the same day someone tried to take one of his carrots out of the plastic bag he kept in his knapsack. The man had a fit right there in front of everyone. He started convulsing and then he fell to the ground and kicked his legs and held his stomach like he'd been punched there. He was like that on the ground for two whole hours wailing. We timed him. We thought maybe he'd pass out but he never did. Still, he'd made a spectacle of himself and maybe this was why some of us secretly hated everything about him. Although you cannot discount his attitude and how he thought he was smarter than the rest of us as a reason for why we hated him so. That sort of pomposity is ugly business. If he were that smart he'd be climbing one of those mountains in Asia, telling the little sherpas to fuck off because he didn't need their help, or he'd sleep every night in a park under a cardboard canopy to protect himself from the wind and rain and finally wake up to paint pictures like an epileptic juvenile and then before long die tragically in a seedy hotel room still tied off, the works all splattered about.

Time Without Number

Not too long ago I wanted sex with someone, a person, but now I do not want sex with anyone. I don't want sex with a woman or a man or someone who is both all the time and every day. If someone approached me and said let's please have sex together I'd say not on your life, full stop. I'd add full stop at the end of my reply for emphasis, so there is no room for misinterpretation. I'd say the very idea of sex is repugnant to me now. I can't remember when I stopped wanting to have sex with people and I also can't remember if something happened to me, if I suffered some sort of disappointment or injury. I don't think any of that matters because what good are explanations. Nobody cares about explanations, and I don't blame them for not caring and I don't care or blame myself, either.

Some Other Metal Than Earth

There might still be dirt and air and mountains but it doesn't seem possible if there's no sky up in the sky or no moon hanging in the middle of it. Just as carrots don't seem possible though they grow in the same dirt. But the dirt carrots grow in is called soil and there's likely no soil. There's no way to differentiate dirt from soil, if there is a difference. There's no optimal time to grow carrots in either dirt or soil because there are no seasons. There's no fall and no spring, which is what's best for carrots, but carrots need fertilizer and there's probably no fertilizer.

That Old Time Religion

LIFE WOULD BE EASIER if I were a beautiful woman or if I were rich or healthy or healthy enough to walk down the street without falling over or if I were the office manager of an advertising agency or professional athlete or serial killer or sex therapist or someone who believes in Jesus or Buddha or Idi Amin, and while I can admit that life wouldn't be easier in every way it would be easier in the most important ways and the upshot is I'd trade places with anyone in the world except for my downstairs neighbor, who is both walleyed and sclerotic and listens to godawful dance music at earsplitting volumes.

The Heartbreak of Psoriasis

We looked at each other from across a narrow hallway or what seemed like a narrow hallway. It may've been an amusement park or bank lobby. Vision loss is one of the side effects, and so ocular confusion is to be expected. There were other people occupying the same space, looking at each other, doing what people do in hallways, amusement parks and bank lobbies. That is to say they were conducting the business of their lives. Anyone could see this, if they could see at all, if the accident hadn't totally compromised their vision and they were paying attention. What else do I have to do on a weekday morning. I don't have a job. I had one once, but they told me I didn't have to do that job anymore, that the job had been completed to everyone's satisfaction. I won't say what the job entailed but sometimes I would go to conferences out of town and conduct symposiums on important topics. After doing this for years they gave me a million dollars and sent me home, but not before thanking me for my efforts. They said they couldn't have done it without me, which was true. I was essential then. I am now resting on laurels, which I did every day with gusto until I saw that woman on the other end of the hallway or bank lobby. She resembled a woman I used to know named Sofia who ruined my life. No one knew about Sofia because I like to suffer in silence but then I eventually told my parents. I call my parents every two or three years to check in, and when I told them about Sofia they said they were sorry but what did I know about heartbreak since I didn't have psoriasis. I think both of them had psoriasis and resented me for not having it, too. I always suspected the only reason they had a child was so that he could have psoriasis and they could lock him up in a shed and make fun of him.

Another thing I can't be too sure about is the person on the other end of that narrow hallway. It's possible it wasn't Sofia, but rather a man. But if it was, in fact, a man, this man had the most delicate features and lustrous hair yet featured on a male human being. It's possible this man was once a woman or was a woman who was once a man and for a second I wanted sex with this person. But there wasn't time for sex and this wasn't the place for it, either. So there we were, looking at each other from across this bank lobby, and a decision had to be made because if you don't make a decision when it comes time to make one you might as well give up and go home forever. It doesn't matter if the decision is wrongheaded or right, so long as you go all the way with it. And so this is what I did and why I'm talking about it now. All of it comes back to the accident, to them giving me the million dollars for my essential efforts and sending me home to rest on my laurels with gusto. Or it goes back to the shed and my parents with psoriasis, depending on how you look at it.

Of course, some people think they gave me the million dollars and sent me home solely because of the accident, as a way of appeasing me, as a way of shutting me up. I don't mind telling you that I consider this horse-and-buggy thinking and shall not dignify it with any sort of counter or denial.

Truth to Power

I CAN'T REMEMBER if life was easier when I was a beautiful woman, which I've been more than once, and I can't remember how I was treated or what I accomplished given that power and privilege or what I endured due to the disadvantage and burden and I can't say I'm looking forward to being a beautiful woman again but I can't say I look forward to anything except for the French toast at my dead brother's restaurant.

Why the Noise Machine Never Works Anymore

THERE IS A WHITE NOISE SETTING and another labeled celestial sounds. I don't know what celestial sounds are supposed to sound like because do the heavens ever make a sound. Maybe when a star explodes, what they call a supernova, I think. But there was no sound when the sky fell four years ago, not even the sound of people screaming and getting crushed to death. This is probably the closest we'll get to a supernova unless the sun explodes, which probably won't happen for a few more years. After the sky fell down there were shards all over the streets so you had to be careful. I cut myself two or three times walking around outside, which is why it's always better to stay home with the noise machine on. The other settings include stream and summer night, which I think means crickets and bullfrogs and related creatures calling out to each other. What they say is come on over and fuck me or kill me or kill me and then fuck me you crazy demented savages, every last one of you.

People Say What, Eat Sandwiches, Watch Television

If you make the mistake of having sex with another person stop yourself at once and apologize. Say to that person I am profoundly sorry for my behavior. Tell them it is inexcusable. Do not wait for the other person to respond because they might forgive you or try to convince you they were not offended by the sex and in fact would like for it to continue. Or years later they might say the sex wasn't consensual and you took advantage because even though they said yes that sounds wonderful they didn't actually mean it and you should've known better. This is why it's best to never consort with anyone at any time. Instead bid them a pleasant good evening and then never have anything to do with this person for the rest of everyone's lives.

An Old Man Said to Me

WHEN PEOPLE SAY what's the story or what's happening you should say what's the difference in return. Do not worry what time of day it is or if you're tired. Be like Sister, who doesn't even have a clock on the wall. What does Sister do all day but sleep and do dishes with cold water. You don't need a clock for those activities. While you are sleeping people will eat sandwiches and watch television. Sometimes they go to the doctor or for a drive in the country. They go to the doctor because they think they might have cancer and they go for a drive in the country because they have nothing better to do. This is why time doesn't matter, and as a case in point you can mention daylight savings time and how it's a sham. How is time real when it keeps changing twice a year. They want to know what is happening, what is doing, what you have been up to. Tell them what do you know. Tell them you have been eating sandwiches and watching television like everyone else. Tell them you like being naked and walk around naked all day long and if they have an issue with that then you don't know what. They'll ask what's the problem or what's the matter. Tell them you dream lives though not your own. Tell them you're not sure who the people are in your dreams. They always try to kill you but sometimes you outsmart them and wake up before anything bad happens. Then you go to the bathroom and empty your bladder. Tell them that it's all because of your bladder, tell them that's the main problem. Tell them it might be cancer, but you don't know. The doctor won't tell you without a biopsy and you do not want a biopsy for the pain, but you know that it runs in your family so you're pretty sure you're doomed. Then tell them you can't drink milk or eat ice cream anymore because you've grown to be lactose intolerant. They'll ask if that's the God's honest truth. Tell them how should you know, you're not religious.

The people who say what to you like this, most speak their own languages. A lot of them come from where the water is bad and the people want out. Places like Poland and Guatemala and Michigan. The people from these places are troubled, their languages incomprehensible. Even still try to make sense of them. Listen for familiar words, sounds. Always look people in the face when they talk in their languages. Say what to them and they'll say what back. Maintain eye contact. Affect a facial gesture that resembles concern or empathy. Remember what that old dead actor once said about acting.

Soon it will be time to go and everyone knows it. They'll thank you for your patience and then ask what you will do with the rest of the day. Start by thanking them for the society and tell them you should clean your house because it is filthy and you will take off your clothes so that you're naked and you should go to the doctor because of your bladder but you are tired and want to go to bed so this is what you tell them. Tell them you will dream them later but promise not to kill me. Tell them it's because of my bladder that people want to kill me. Look them straight in the face and ask if they'd give a drowning man a glass of water and then walk away before they have a chance to answer.

Won't See Another One

Tax Returns

It was yesterday when they shot him outside his home. It was still dark out and it was raining and all the neighbors were getting ready for work and they shot him in front of everybody.

They'd followed him all night from the restaurant to the bar to the skating rink to the hotel and then back home. This is when they rushed out of their car and shot him twelve times in the back.

It was now morning and it was still dark and the rain made the sidewalk slick and dangerous and two people slipped and fell and injured themselves. But this was before they shot him so no one remembers that two people got hurt that morning by falling on the sidewalk.

It was one hundred years ago when they shot him yesterday outside his home in New York City. People were getting ready for work as it was a workday and this one had a meeting and that one had a presentation and this other one had a route and that other one had a double shift at the plant but it was going to be time and a half.

It was outside his building. It was early.

This is the same building where all the neighbors lived and where two of them fell on the sidewalk because it was raining. One of them wound up in the same hospital they later brought him to after he was shot.

This one, the one who wound up in the same hospital, he needed four stitches for the gash on his forehead. The scar was something this one would talk about for the rest of his life, always in relation to how it was the same morning of the shooting.

All of the neighbors are decent people who work honest jobs. Almost every neighbor files a tax return, though some take extensions and others forget altogether and a year or two later they are audited and it's a disaster as they don't keep records or receipts and no one knows what to do about it.

Some of the neighbors have tuberculosis and others have shingles or scurvy or rickets and still others suffer from all manner of troubling ailments and afflictions, but the two people who fell that morning are fine now.

It was early in the morning and in front of all the neighbors when they shot him outside in the rain. One of the neighbors was a woman named Manny. Everyone thought it strange that there was a woman named Manny and that she worked for the railroad and if she wasn't famous for her paella then she was famous for knitting afghans and that she coughed all the time.

When people talked about Manny they talked about her paella and her afghans and that her name was Manny and that she coughed all the time.

Manny was the one who called the ambulance after the shooting and she was the one who was interviewed on television about what she saw, which was everything.

She saw the ambush and the shooting and how he crumpled and staggered and fell to the ground.

I wasn't the one who shot him and I wasn't the one who slipped and fell on the sidewalk.

I wasn't the one who shot him yesterday outside his home in New York City and I wasn't the one who got audited a year later after failing to file a tax return. But it was me who shot him.

I'm not saying I was the one who shot him yesterday outside his home, but it was me who shot him one hundred years ago. It was in the evening time or it was early morning because it was dark out. It was one or two lifetimes ago. All the neighbors were outside eating paella in the rain or getting ready for work or falling down on the sidewalk.

It was all of us who shot him yesterday outside his home in New York City one hundred years ago. It was every person that ever lived that shot him.

There are sick people living in this building.

I've never met a woman named Manny, but my grandmother knitted afghans and there's a photograph of me as an infant in which I appear to be asleep with one draped all over me.

Folders

One man says to the other, we are speaking in hypotheticals now. We all know this can't happen in real life.

The man is referring to his marriage, the one he's been in for twelve years. Before that he drifted in and out, found himself in a few bad situations with the wrong kind of people.

Once he was involved with a woman who liked to commemorate these bad situations with tattoos. The first one was an ambigram on her wrist that read "I'm fine" or "Save me" depending on how you looked at it. The next time he tried not to notice it from any angle.

The woman was known as Sister and had a best friend named Sofia. He didn't like anything about this Sofia. He didn't like that she always carried with her a leather satchel that bisected her breasts and wore copious amounts of eye shadow and he also didn't like how she spelled her name. Sister would call and suggest the three of them go out to dinner, that they hike up some mountain in Vermont or go on vacation somewhere warm.

The other man is only there in relation to the first man. He has no life of his own, not to speak of. Yes, he sleeps in a queen-size bed and eats yogurt with granola every morning, but otherwise, there is nothing noteworthy about him.

Once the other man hired a cleaning woman to clean his apartment. Both of them remained clothed the entire time and this is something the other man will never get over.

The first man says, in real life this is someone who needs help.

The other man says, I won't take this abuse much longer.

The day began as most days do, in the morning. The first man woke early, made breakfast and then ate it. He looked out the window and considered a running jump. He watched the television news. Somewhere in Asia people were being wiped out by a sequence of natural disasters. On the home front, some locals got into trouble with the police and it turned into a free-for-all.

The man is married to a woman who folds everything. She folds towels and sheets and paper napkins, folds plastic bags, cardboard boxes, anything that can be folded. Sometimes, after sex, she tucks her legs into her chest and folds herself up right there in bed.

The first man says, we call in the Marines, the Red Cross.

The other man says, it's all too much.

The first man says, it's indisputable.

The man has height and weight and a steady income. He lives a daily life. He drives a reliable car, one with four doors and two speakers. He uses his fingers to eat, shave, and write notes to his wife. The notes concern the locals or what he hears on the news. His wife folds the notes up neatly, sometimes making paper airplanes out of them.

The two men are friends. They share values. They have history between them. They counsel each other on matters great and small.

They mean almost nothing to each other.

Meaning if one or the other disappeared, neither would take notice.

It's possible the first one is named Manny and the other man has a different name.

The first man continues and says, What I want now is I want to go outside and play football. I haven't played football in years, but years ago I would play all the time. I was good.

The men are eating and drinking. They are in a restaurant. There are other people also eating and drinking. The men do not pay any attention to the other people, who pay the men no attention either.

At home the man keeps a bouquet of paper airplanes in a flowerpot. He never opens the airplanes to see what is written inside.

The first man says, I want to see my breath disappear in the air and lose sensation in my limbs. I want to go out for a pass and scream bloody murder when the ball hits me in the chest. I want to fall to the ground, desperate for wind. I want the other players to huddle over me. I want there to be genuine concern.

The other man says, my parents never let me play football. He says, instead they locked me up in a shed out back and did unspeakable things to me.

The first man says, then I want to limp home after the game and feel sore. I want to take off my sweatshirt and drape it on the sofa to dry. He says, is this too much to ask of the world?

The other man says, because you married a folder it probably is.

The first man, Manny to most of his friends, thinks about this, the implications. He thinks about his wife and what she might be folding now while he is out to dinner.

The man wants another drink and plans to order one. He will probably have another after that. Then he will probably go home, unless his friend wants another. The man will be open to suggestion.

This is when loud sirens go off, which indicate there is a tsunami warning and everyone should head for higher ground. This restaurant is in a coastal evacuation area but no one has ever had to evacuate. Somewhere on the other side of the world there was an earthquake and now everyone is about to drown.

Neither man reacts to the sirens. They look at each other as though nothing is about to happen because nothing ever happens to either of them.

They both will be dead within hours.

One will drown on the way home and the other inside a tavern where he decided he needed another drink and perhaps the company of someone who might resist the temptation to fold whatever crossed her path.

The first man, probably named Manny but it's possible his name is Bill or Sharon, doesn't actually want to play football and isn't sure why he's indicated otherwise. He never played football as a younger man and certainly wasn't good at it. Maybe he tried once or twice, but he couldn't run, couldn't tackle or block, couldn't catch or throw. His friend is a casual fan meaning that he's no fan at all, and he never thinks about the game and doesn't even watch it on television.

The World Must Be Peopled

Go to a place called Luck and try to make a life there. Learn a trade. Be a plumber like the guy in that movie or an electrician like the guy in that other movie or be a carpenter like Jesus even though people say Jesus couldn't have been a carpenter because there was a paucity of trees in Galilee so he must've been a mason.

An Attempt at Human Relations

The woman invited the man over for dinner and a movie and while they did eat dinner, she'd made a roast chicken with potatoes and string beans, they skipped the movie and instead started talking about their lives: what they were doing for work, where they'd travelled, things of this nature. She wasn't sure if this was a date, as she hadn't seen the man in well over a year. She wasn't sure if he was single or seeing someone or what she might expect from him, if he'd make a pass at her. When they'd first met he pursued her diligently, attempted to woo her in an old-fashioned way she wasn't used to, as he brought her flowers and held her hand while they walked to dinner. But this was three years ago now and she couldn't quite remember what had happened between them or how it happened. She was mindful of living in the present now. First they discussed tennis, which had been a common interest and how they'd met three years ago. They had played together a few times and it was always an enjoyable experience, as he was a good player who didn't take the game too seriously. He didn't want to keep score or play games and was content with rallying back and forth at a leisurely pace. She knew he was better than her, stronger and faster, because she'd seen him play against men and it was clear he wasn't hitting the ball as hard as he could, which she considered gentlemanly, but he also wasn't disrespectful or treating her like a novice. It was clear to him that she could play, had a strong and consistent forehand and an entirely respectable two-fisted backhand that she wasn't as confident in so she would run around it whenever possible. She lamented that she hadn't been able to play as much lately due to a hamstring injury, which was slow to heal. She'd taken solace in her yoga practice, which she does nearly every day. She suggested he do yoga and he said he wasn't flexible and she said yoga helps with flexibility but she knew she wasn't going to convince him to try yoga. He wasn't the type to do yoga and she knew he wasn't the type to get talked into anything. She wasn't sure what type he was, but could tell what he wasn't into and she wasn't sure she was attracted to him and she wasn't sure why that was the case. They'd met three years ago at the tennis courts and he asked her out that very evening. He suggested a drink or dinner and asked for her phone number or email address. She can't remember how he contacted her that first time because they'd communicated both via email and text message. He was always flirtatious in either medium and would suggest she *holler* when she was ready to get together. She actually enjoyed typing the words, *I'm hollering*, and she enjoyed his responses, too, which were always quick to arrive and seemed genuine. She remembered thinking that perhaps this was a red flag, that maybe he was too eager. She even suggested that perhaps he shouldn't reply quite so promptly to a text message or email. She said there was something about mystery and elusiveness that was appealing to her. He responded that he wasn't into games and didn't like to play any. He said he was too old for such things. They had sort of dated when they'd first met but it was fraught with uncertainty, full of stops and starts, and it ended abruptly after a night when they tried to have sex but couldn't. Something wasn't right between the two of them sexually, there was a lack of chemistry. She'd had this issue before with men, had been hesitant when it came to new lovers, uncertain what to do or how to do it. She's always been in her head when it comes to sex and dating and this is something she has talked about in therapy for years. She sees her therapist weekly and credits her with the extraordinary improvements she's made in her life, including those in the sexual arena, but it has yet to bear any tangible fruit. Like every other person who spends years in therapy she still has the same exact problems, makes the same mistakes. The only difference is she has a new language to talk about it after the fact. She once considered making an appointment with a sex therapist but decided against it. This was after someone called her frigid, and she never spoke to that man again, throwing him out of her house before he could get fully dressed. This was something she'd tried to work on, as well, a suffer-no-creeps-or-fools mindset while constantly asserting herself regardless of circumstance. It was true she was working out who she was as a sexual being, as she didn't think of herself as especially sexy or sexual, though she was good-looking and in great physical shape and possessed what she considered a typical female libido, although perhaps it was waning now that she was in her early forties. As for the man, he was charming and respectful and quick-witted and handsome in a rugged, athletic way. He was short but well-proportioned and muscular. She thought she should be attracted to him and wanted to be attracted to him but couldn't decide if she actually was, but maybe there was fear and uncertainty and some kind of inherited repression getting in the way, and she tried not to think about any of this as they had dinner and talked about tennis. Then the conversation moved to vacations and what was going on with their respective families and careers, he a lecturer who went around the country giving talks on the environment and she a private school Spanish teacher who was considering a move into administration. She said to him I'm not sure what we're doing here and he said that makes two of us. Then he said I wouldn't mind kissing you and she said then you probably should and so they kissed and it was enjoyable and passionate for a minute or two. This is when he tried to remove her top and she asked him to go slower, which he did. They kept on kissing and after a few minutes he asked if it was okay now and she laughed and said yes and he removed her top and started kissing her breasts and belly, up and down, slowly and tenderly. She enjoyed the feeling of his kissing, but it also tickled her and she was trying hard to suppress the laughter. This is when he stopped and asked if he could take a shower. She didn't think he was serious about wanting to take a shower. She said, for real, a shower and he answered that he was, in fact, for real. She walked down the hall and fetched him a fresh towel from the linen closet and directed him to the shower. She told him how to turn the handle all the way to the left to get the water hot and left him alone. She went back into the living room and picked up a magazine. She couldn't decide if this was off-putting, but she figured he was sweating and wanted to make himself fresh for her. She noticed he'd wiped his brow with a handkerchief during dinner, but she neglected to ask if he was uncomfortable, if it was too warm. She is unpracticed as a host but would like to do more entertaining in the future, be it for potential dates or friends. She tried to concentrate on the magazine article, which concerned the forthcoming presidential election and the field of candidates who were sometimes inspiring but all the time tedious. This is also what she thought of her students and her job as a whole, which is why she was considering a move out of the classroom and into administration. The administrative position would likely prove tedious, too, with its own particular dramas and complications, but at least it would be something different and she wouldn't have to be in front of a roomful of ill-mannered children four times a day, going over conjugations and sentence structure and saying Me llamo Miss So and So and quantos años tienes y pues nada y nada. She wondered what he was doing in the shower, if maybe he was masturbating because he'd mentioned he enjoys it as a routine activity, then realized he probably wouldn't do that with her waiting for him. For a quick minute she considered joining him in the shower, figured it would be received as a sexy maneuver, but she wasn't the type to make such bold gestures and she didn't enjoy the prospect of sex in the shower, if that's what he'd expect or propose. Also, the man hadn't seen her naked yet, and she didn't want to be naked in front of him under the bathroom light. The first time they tried to have sex and failed the lights were off, so he couldn't see the look on her face and vice versa.

She put the magazine down on the coffee table but picked it back up again when she heard the bathroom door opening. He returned to the living room wrapped in the towel she gave him from the linen closet and sat down next to her. The woman thought it a good idea to pretend not to notice. She thought it would be playful, the insouciance. She remembered another time when she'd hosted a man on a date, but this time the man had bussed in from Baltimore for the occasion and was slated to spend the entire weekend with her. They'd met at a conference and had hit it off and exchanged information about six months prior to these plans unexpectedly coming to fruition. She figured she'd never hear from him again, as they hadn't so much as kissed during their brief time together at the conference, but he reached out via social media and they began a correspondence that turned flirtatious and after they each invited the other up or down for the weekend he called her bluff and showed up on a Friday evening. That first night together they went to dinner and talked about their lives as people do on first dates and at the end of the evening, she showed him to the guest room where she'd made up the bed for him. They shared a gentle kiss goodnight and she went to bed thinking it was a good first date and sure it was weird that her date was spending the night, one tiny room away from her own, but they lived three hours apart and there was no other choice. The next day they went to a museum and she took him on a tour of the city and by the end of the evening she found herself back at the door of his bedroom, giving him another chaste kiss goodnight. She realized the man was either shy or awkward and reluctant to put a move on her, which she sort of wanted him to do and was sort of relieved that he didn't. Later that night, though, she knocked on his door and climbed into bed with him, where he was naked and awake. She made a joke that she knew she'd get him naked and made a gesture of patting her own back. Then they made out and he caressed her back and buttocks and breasts through her nightgown, but never made a move to remove it or reach up underneath it. She never touched him while they kissed and hugged under the covers, so she didn't know if he'd had an erection or not. Still he didn't put his hands near her genitals or try to guide her hands toward his and she wasn't one to make that sort of first move, even though she thought her going into his room and climbing into bed with him qualified as a first move. They never did have any kind of sex that night or any other and never saw each other again romantically after that, although they did run into each other the following year at the same conference and exchanged pleasantries and vague plans to reconnect once they got home.

This night the man in the towel picked up on her cue and retrieved a different magazine from the coffee table and started to page through it. This went on for a minute before they both broke out laughing. Then he leaned into her and they started kissing in earnest and it was clear he was somehow invigorated by the shower as he removed the top that she had put back on and started to take down her shorts. The woman tried to resist, but he looked up at her with big eyes and said it was okay, that they'd go slow and take their time and wouldn't do anything she wasn't comfortable with, but they should be naked together now. She liked the way he'd framed it and looked him in the eye and they both smiled. She shimmied out of her shorts and underwear and led him into the bedroom. She wanted everything to be okay and she wanted to be normal and she wanted to have sex like everyone else in the world. But the same problem happened as before, as the man couldn't get aroused, or rather, he would get aroused but quickly lose his erection. This is when he changed tack and begin kissing her all over desperately, working his way up and down her body and between her legs to pleasure her, all the while manipulating his penis in an attempt to regain his erection. She wished he wouldn't do that, wished it wasn't that important to him, but she knew that men are sensitive to this sort of thing and she wanted to help him, but felt herself recoil at the prospect of touching him there or going down on him. A few minutes later, when he suggested she do just that, she wanted to say no but she wasn't sure why, he'd done the same to her and he was sweet and kind and gentle and as far as penises go he had a nice one, it was actually pretty, if such a thing is possible, and she didn't know what was wrong with her. She thought of her friends who had no problems with sex, who could do anything and everything, but as much as she tried it wasn't in her, she was different, locked up somehow, inhibited, and she wasn't sure why, though she suspected it had to do with her first experiences which were crude and unsatisfying, and maybe it had to do with her mother who never talked about sex and seemed entirely asexual and disapproving of sex, and it was also her body and how unhappy she was with it. Sure she was taut and lean and had shapely legs and buttocks, which is where the tennis and yoga had yielded obvious results, but she was always embarrassed about her breasts, which fit into an A cup bra with room to spare as there was hardly any breast tissue surrounding her nipples. Still, the man appreciated her there and kissed and gently touched her nipples and breasts and never said a single word about them, though others in the past hadn't been so kind. So she took him in her mouth and he grew hard and they quickly changed positions and he seemed in great haste, but when it came time for the man to enter her he couldn't. She'd readied herself for that initial spasm of pain and hoped it would subside quickly, but they never got that far. After two or three attempts at penetration the man fell back on his haunches and said, I can't believe this, I'm sorry. No one said anything for a solid minute until the man got up and did a lap around the room. This is when he collapsed in bed next to her and said that this happens all the time, that they had to get used to each other, that it would be better when they tried again. The woman agreed with him and tried not to think of this as a failure, tried not to think she was a failure and would never be able to have sex with anyone again, so she concentrated on everything that was good about the evening, the chicken and the banter and the magazine business, and wondered if they would indeed try again and when that might be, and then she thought about her morning yoga class and how she promised to meet her friend Esperanza for coffee beforehand. She didn't know if he was going to spend the night or if she should invite him to stay, but he said he needed to wake up early as he got up from the bed and started dressing. She told him that was just as well because she had an early coffee date and it was important she keep it because her friend Esperanza had been going through a hard time recently and needed to talk.

Sometimes in the Morning

If you make the mistake of remaining in a flood zone after the authorities ordered everyone to evacuate and you see the waters rushing and rising all around you do not retrieve the rowboat or kayak from the shed behind your house and paddle your way to safety. Do not climb up to the roof of your house so that a helicopter can rescue you. At this juncture in one's life it is imperative to face reality and drown with a measure of dignity like the captain who refuses to abandon ship. Perhaps there will be time to write a last will and testament so that your loved ones can find it when the floodwaters recede and they sift through the wreckage. Be sure to seal the document in plastic to protect it from damage.

I Would Not Feel So All Alone

Manny actually believed he'd lived past lives and told me the story of how he came to be one of Jesus's disciples. He was playing handball with James or Thomas when this short, stocky man who turned out to be Jesus showed up and said I got next. Manny said that's fine, but we're playing two out of three and Jesus said he had no problem waiting his turn. Manny wound up winning the rubber match, which was a barn burner, but by then Jesus had wandered off. They saw him later that night and shared tankards of ale at an underground tavern, and by morning Manny was an apostle. They toured most of Galilee, playing three shows a night, until there were some creative differences and lineup changes and Manny quit to start a solo career. It wasn't until two or three hundred years later when Manny came across a band of peasants praising his name that he learned what had happened to Jesus and he couldn't believe any of it.

When You're Young and Able

This is what happens; we wake up, sometimes in the morning. There is nothing to do.

When there is nothing to do and nowhere to go you can do anything or go anywhere. This is why we go to the beach so we can watch the waves pound the shore. We find it soothing, the repetition and predictability. We wonder where the waves started, if that can be measured. We wonder if the waves began on the other side of the world or only a hundred yards offshore. We hope to see a tsunami, a titanic wave higher than a skyscraper. We'd like to see some fool try to surf that wave and then we'd like to see a team of lifeguards run into the water and drag that surfer to shore after he's been knocked unconscious. This is what we think about when we wake up in the morning and go to the beach to watch the waves pound the shore. We could eat breakfast, sure, but then what. We would only have to eat lunch a few hours later and then what after that. Anyone can see what we mean, where we're going. This is what happens every day and how it happens every day, starting when we wake up, sometimes in the morning, so it's no different. There's time to think about people drowning, about someone the ocean got the better of, someone who caught a lungful of water and became disoriented. We know what it's like to be underwater unable to surface. We were inside a womb like everyone else. That's what it's like in there; it's like drowning for nine months straight. This is why we haven't been in the water since, because who wants to go through that again. Maybe someday, though, if we think about it, which we do sometimes, in the morning, if we wake up, meaning we can't discount it, wanting to swim. There is something elegant about swimming, like gliding through the air, like floating weightlessly through the astral plane. So what if you're likely to drown and miss a skinny eighteen-year-old lifeguard beating your chest with spindly arms, while another blows bad air into your mouth and counts one two three four. As if all that adds up to something worthwhile, as if that can save you.

What There Is to Understand about Drowning

Because what we are talking about is a structure, an object made of earthly matter, be it wood or steel or aluminum, although there might be some question as to what constitutes earthly matter and if steel or aluminum qualifies. The indisputable truth is that boats don't drown regardless of composition. People are the ones who drown and this is the difference between boats and people, how you can tell them apart. Something happens to the boat, then the boat takes on water, then it sinks right to the bottom of the ocean where it will remain until the sun finally explodes into a million pieces. One might wonder what happens to the boat, what makes it sink. Let me understand that it doesn't matter. If there are people on the boat they can try to keep the boat from sinking, although their efforts are always futile. Say one of them is named Manny and the other Esperanza because why shouldn't their names be Manny and Esperanza. Understand that Manny and Esperanza can take measures. They can use words like bow, stern, starboard, and port, which means front, rear, right, and left. They might even bail water and put on lifejackets. This is when Manny and Esperanza float around until someone comes by to pick them up.

We don't know what Manny and Esperanza might discuss while

they are floating in the ocean like this because it doesn't matter. Say Manny asks, what do you have tomorrow and Esperanza answers, my dignity. Then what?

The ones who come by to help are called rescuers and they know to come by because they have been signaled. They are signaled through direct radio contact or by Morse code. Morse code, in telegraphy, is a series of dots and dashes that indicate different letters of the alphabet. S.O.S is the most famous code sent, which means Save our Ship, although some people say it doesn't actually mean Save our Ship. Two of these people are named Manny and Esperanza and this tells you everything you need to know about them. Rescuers are given positions of longitude and latitude and this is how they know where to go to save Manny and Esperanza, who are still out there floating on the water in their lifejackets and talking about God knows what. They say that rats are the first ones off a sinking ship, but unless they are extraordinary swimmers it does them little good so we will not discuss or try to understand the rats. The people rescued, in this particular case Manny and Esperanza, are called survivors. They are called the lucky ones because they have survived and the unlucky ones are called victims and these include Sofia and Benjamin and Tanya. These are the people who are subject to float around with no one coming by to pick them up. We will never know what happened to them but we can assume that sharks attacked them or the sun beat down on them or it was freezing cold and they caught what is called hypothermia. Hypothermia is a state of reduced body temperature wherein all bodily functions are slowed.

People can either be rescued or recovered, survivors or victims. However, there are victims who are never recovered. These are the people lost at sea. There are songs written about them and they are called dirges. Boats are also lost at sea, and they are mentioned in the same songs. Let me understand to everyone that while dirge sounds like a nautical term, it isn't. But drowning almost always happens in the water, unless we're talking about secondary drowning which we can't get into because it won't help anyone. Drowning is for people who can't swim or who can no longer swim due to injury or exhaustion, or people who choose not to swim. Something happens, then they take on water, then they drown. The water can be deep or shallow, rough or calm. Water fills the lungs, making life at first difficult, then impossible to sustain. Then they sink to the bottom of the ocean, where their bodies will remain until the sun explodes into a million pieces or the ocean dries up and turns into a desert like the Sahara did ages ago. I'm here to tell you I was there when it happened and I couldn't believe what I was seeing.

The Polar Ice Caps and How They've Melted

GRADUALLY, then all at once.

R under Multiplication

People have always confused me, what they say, how they behave. I've tried being patient, thinking it all the way through, the way I was with Esperanza, but it's of no use. I'm incapable of figuring anything or anyone out.

Someone once said to me, suppose that R was closed under multiplication. I was minding my own business at the time, which is why it was appalling.

Whether they're ones I'm related to or have myself pressed up against in some way, or even people I work with, it doesn't matter. They're all goners.

The trouble is I'm human like most people and sometimes I have human needs. The ones that keep you up at night and have you reaching between your legs.

This is only one reason leaving the house is a bad idea.

The best thing you can say about me is I have a sister who does the dishes after I've cooked everyone dinner.

Otherwise, I have trouble falling asleep, then I have trouble staying asleep, then I have trouble waking up.

There is never anyone next to me when I do wake up, though years ago Esperanza would've been next to me, but she left when I was looking the other way.

She could be anywhere in the world and it wouldn't matter.

I don't like to think about where she could be or my sister or the dishes or what's between my legs or why I have trouble sleeping. The list of things I don't like to think about includes breakfast, lunch, and dinner, too.

I never thought I was the R that person referred to in her theoretical problem, but

I do believe I am closed under multiplication.

The Gun Is Where Any Could Find It

You live in America so there are guns. Always have your guns with you, take them with you to school and to work and to the movies and to the mall and to the barber or beauty shop. Have a gun for your right hand and a gun for your left hand and keep one tucked inside a boot or shoe. Only a certain kind of person looks at a lowercase r and sees a gun. Always be that kind of person.

Sister in Basement, Manny Again Elsewhere

Manny would love for the woman behind him to shut the fuck up. Manny is on the train ride home and the woman behind him is on the same train. The difference is Manny wants the woman to shut the fuck up and the woman wants nothing from Manny. She doesn't even know he's there, that he exists, that he's a person.

Sofia and Esperanza are tangled up two doors down from where Sister is in the basement doing dishes with cold water.

It's been one month since Sofia and Esperanza met each other, so it was okay now for Sofia to clean and redecorate Esperanza's apartment. Sofia said she'd wanted to do this since the first time she came over, the night they met at someone's going-away party.

They've both forgotten who was going away or where it was they were going, now that they are so caught up in each other.

Sofia said there was something bad wrong with Esperanza. She said she could see spending the rest of her life with her, but that didn't mean something wasn't wrong. Esperanza told her it was true, that she was allergic to dust, that if she tried dusting she could have an anaphylactic reaction and die.

Sofia said, that doesn't sound right to me, and started in with a dust rag on one of the end tables. She said, this is me after dance class. I always have an abundance of energy.

Esperanza told her she wasn't kidding. She said, my throat could close and I could suffocate and die. Sofia looked at Esperanza straight in the eye, did a pirouette. She said, you poor thing.

Manny and Sister don't know who they are, Sofia and Esperanza, and have never met them.

But they are all connected by proximity and certain relationship dynamics and unbeknownst to all they were in the same restaurant three weeks ago late Friday night. Manny and Sister were having dinner after a bad movie as Sofia and Esperanza were finishing a dessert of flourless chocolate cake.

Manny doesn't want to turn around, doesn't want to know if the woman is one seat behind him or two. He doesn't want to know what she looks like, doesn't want to see what she's wearing.

Perhaps the woman is not going home or perhaps she will be abducted before she gets there.

Two women and one child have gone missing in the last month, and everyone is worried about who might be next.

Everyone is making sure to have their guns with them when they leave the house in the morning. Some carry it in a holster and others have it tucked inside a belt buckle or boot or shoe.

Sister is in the basement, washing dishes with cold water. She doesn't know where Manny is, but she thinks he might be at work or on the train. It's also true she doesn't care.

The woman is on the phone and two seats behind Manny. She says he doesn't understand because he's a man. Then she says, don't think about Benjamin for the next twenty-four hours.

It's unclear who this woman might be talking with and what it has to do with Manny.

That Sofia and Esperanza are tangled up two doors down doesn't mean anything in this context, as it's almost certain that the woman is not talking to either Sofia or Esperanza.

This means it's impossible to know who Benjamin is or why anyone should care about him.

Sister did know a Benjamin in grade school but it's probably a different Benjamin.

Manny has never known a Benjamin, has never even met one.

Grade school Benjamin wore parachute pants and was cross-eyed. He had both a trick knee and plantar wart. The Benjamin being discussed by the woman sitting behind Manny has no such afflictions and it turns out is both stylish and athletic.

But Benjamin doesn't matter at all, regardless of his appearance. The woman talking about Benjamin doesn't matter and Sofia and Esperanza don't matter, either.

Because this has to be about Manny and Sister and what might happen between them moving forward. It's also about everything that's already happened between them and against them.

What's happened is so mystifying it would be impossible for anyone to articulate it without the benefit of hindsight or omniscience.

We should wait to see if anything worthwhile transpires for these two and if we never again return to Manny and Sister then so be it.

Conversation Over Mixed Signals

Be prepared for me to be awful. This is what the woman next to Manny says out loud to the woman next to her. Manny doesn't know either of these women and doesn't care to. He has known enough women for one lifetime. He is on his way to the doctor because he can't sleep through the night without waking up ten times to empty his bladder. He is certain one day he won't wake up because he will have dehydrated and lapsed into a coma during sleep. He once told a romantic interest that should he lapse into a coma while they had sex, she should continue regardless. He said he'd like the same courtesy, but only if she consented. He can't remember what happened next. Manny knows there is something wrong with him and he's almost certain that it's cancer. He's tried everything you could think of, like spending a whole day without drinking a single glass of water even though he knows it isn't good to go a whole day without water. He's seen this show on TV where two idiots get put someplace awful and told they have to stay there for three weeks. They have no food or water or shelter or clothes. Sometimes they go days and days without water and it's funny to watch them bitch and moan about the heat and the humidity and how they're starving and thirsty. Manny doesn't feel sorry for these people because they signed up for this.

Manny didn't sign up to go to the bathroom every fifteen minutes and that's the difference. Manny is an innocent victim and deserves sympathy or pity. But he understands nobody cares, and so Manny keeps it to himself. Sometimes he thinks it's his diet, which is terrible. He eats only fast food because he doesn't have time for anything else. This is why he goes to one of two fast food restaurants every day. What's funny is the kids that work there act as if they don't recognize him in either place. When he wakes up in the middle of the night to go to the bathroom, he sometimes turns on the light and looks in the mirror and he doesn't recognize himself, either. He doesn't blame the kids for treating him like a stranger and he doesn't blame the woman next to him for being awful. Manny doesn't recognize either woman, but one is Esperanza and the other is Sofia. They are on their way to a new restaurant that everyone says is the best thing going. For Manny's part, he doesn't blame anyone for anything, except maybe the doctor later, who he's sure can't and won't help him.

For Man Is a Giddy Thing

SISTER SMOTHERED THE BABY to keep it quiet because everyone had paid good money to hear the guest speaker. What we're saying is it was not premeditated or malicious. It's true that it wasn't Sister's baby and never could be. Sister doesn't have any children herself and in fact is barren. Someone said she had a hostile womb, and it makes sense, even though she does have a warm and motherly look about her. One assumes this is why she was entrusted with the baby once the lecture began, which was a symposium on the polar ice caps and how they're melting. This was the fourth year in a row the conference was held in this city, but the first time the baby attended. It's also true we don't know who the parents were or how the baby came to be in the lecture hall. Some speculated it was the guest speaker's baby and this could well be true. The guest speaker seemed upset when Sister smothered the baby, though it was for her own benefit and that of those in her audience. The speaker was named Tanya, and she gave a talk on the ice caps and electric fans and sex and gender fluidity and the surprising manner in which these topics are connected. She said something about fractal geometry or chaos theory and then something else about Hegelian meta duality. We weren't paying close attention, and for that we apologize. We had other things on our mind, all of which are tedious and not worth discussing.

Midnight, Assist Our Moan

SURROUNDED BY FAMILY AND FRIENDS, including son and daughter, one who works as a dental hygienist and the other a college student in the Midwest, Esperanza Gonzalez y Martinez passed away due to complications after a yearlong bout with non-Hodgkin's lymphoma. She is survived by the aforementioned son and daughter and her ex-husband, notorious blues musician Blind Manny Martinez.

Park Like Smith

I WANT EVERYONE in the world to know what my life is like now, how I go through my day.

I am all the time hopeless but for hope.

I am all the time foolish and tired.

Every day I check the mail. Every day I listen for the phone.

The thinking is maybe there will be news.

Otherwise, I listen to myself do nothing. I listen to how awful it is.

How it sounds is the occasional cough, the odd crackle from a knee-cap when rising from bed, the loud crunching when I eat my carrots, a muted exhalation after masturbating.

Outside, there's a fog.

The day is yellow.

It's always freezing too cold or Death Valley hot.

I look out the window and never see you on the street anymore.

I don't see you walking your dog and I don't see you rending your garments.

Perhaps you didn't mean I should remain in my apartment with the curtains drawn when you told me we should wait for a better time to get together.

I have left my bedroom several times in the past two weeks, but have been out of doors only once.

What happened was I went for a walk.

I was out of carrots.

Every day I eat my carrots and do the crossword puzzle. What else could I do all day by myself in this awful apartment.

It's true that I masturbate sometimes.

This is like how it was years ago when I was in that place.

I once lived in a room that had in it only a telephone and bed. Sometimes the phone would ring, and I would answer it and talk to whoever was on the other end of the line.

I masturbated every morning in that room and sometimes in the evening, as well, before bed. Sometimes I masturbated because there was nothing else to do. If they'd given me a television to watch I would've watched it and maybe then I would've stopped masturbating all the time. I think they wanted me to keep masturbating which is why they didn't give me a television. I think they watched me to see how many times I could masturbate in a day. I think I was their television is another way of saying it.

There was probably a sofa on the other side of the window where they watched me and compiled data. I think I was part of a study about the relationship between masturbation and the lack of television. It may or may not have had something to do with the phone always ringing, too. Maybe they thought the sound of the phone ringing made me want to masturbate all the time.

The people who watched me were doctors with white coats and clipboards. They were not smart or generous, not like you and me.

I could tell they weren't smart because they weren't good at helping people get better, which is why I was there in the first place.

Maybe I was wired to want to masturbate whenever the phone rang. Whenever I frisked myself, I never did find any wires, but maybe they put the wires on the inside.

This is why I don't have a television in my room, but I do have a telephone because how else would I know if you call me.

I hope you won't mind when you call that I might be in the middle of masturbating or eating carrots or doing the crossword, but I will never do all three at the same time.

As I said before, I had to go out into the world because I was out of carrots.

What happened next was I took a wrong step and hurt my knee again.

I can't describe the pain other than to say I'd like to have died from it. The pain started at the top and then worked its way up and down in every direction. I felt it all the way through to my ankles.

I almost fell to the ground but steadied myself on a bicycle rack.

It was all I could do to make it to the grocer's conscious and ambulatory. I'm sure you didn't see this happen, weren't watching from your bedroom window. Certainly you would've helped me to the grocer.

I did imagine you at your window looking down at me, then coming to my aid right there on the street.

I'm sure you were inside your house waiting for a better time, so I am not angry or resentful.

Part of what was wrong was the noise in my head. The noise in my head was like an awful dial tone from a horrible phone that never shuts off.

I could masturbate and masturbate and still this tone all the time.

It is high-pitched and constant and sounds like the hissing of a poisonous snake and a giant garbage truck grinding on its brakes at the same time.

I asked the doctors to fix it, and they said they couldn't. I asked them if it was cancer, and they said something about your guess and mine.

I do remember thinking that I would not stop masturbating to answer the phone.

Every time I stopped masturbating to answer the phone, I couldn't concentrate on the words coming from the person on the other end and it was awkward.

This is most true if it is my mother on the other end, who went through hell giving birth to me but it wasn't a picnic from my perspective, either.

I think I remember I was born in the middle of a horrible headache.

Why I had this headache is I got stuck in my mother's tubes on the way out.

Mother said the doctors had to go in with pliers to get me out. She said they had to clamp the pliers hard around my head and crushed my skull in the process.

This is why I have headaches all the time.

I had to wear a special helmet whenever I left the house. I would be halfway out the door, and Mother would scream from the kitchen go get your fucking helmet.

I don't have to wear the helmet anymore.

I want you to know that I remember my mother sometimes even

though I try not to.

Every day she would feed me rice and beans and beat me with a switch, so what does that tell you about the woman.

I've been to the grocer's many times, but I still get lost. When I finally find the store, the grocer gives me my carrots for free because he knows what the doctors and my mother did to me all those years ago.

I remember my mother called the grocer Chinese but the grocer says that's a lie. He says his name is Park.

I can't always understand what the grocer says. The first time he said his name was Park I told him to forget about it.

Now it's something like a joke between us.

This is when he gives me my carrots and tells me to go fuck myself.

Then we laugh and laugh.

I can't remember how this started, but I wanted to tell you about my knee.

My knee hurts but that's not even a fraction of what's wrong with me.

When last we parted you said let's wait for a better time, so this is what I'm writing to tell you, that I'm doing what you said, that I'm waiting.

I remain faithful and steadfast.

I await further instructions.

Is Courtesy a Turncoat

WELL YOU WOKE UP this morning and looked out the door, you could tell that old milk cow by the way she lowed.

Entertainment

Look at Manny attempting to woo a much younger woman. Look at him sweating and mopping his brow with a handkerchief while he tries to make conversation. Notice how he sucks in his gut, how he sits on the sofa with his arm draped over the back. What can we say about him that hasn't been said a million times before.

Is This a Better Time

Everyone in this train car is dead or appears dead or is about to die because there's no air to breathe and because it's July and because it's a heat wave and because the weather is going to kill all of us dead and everywhere you go it's a hundred degrees and so you get on a train because you think they'll have air conditioning because this is America and we are taxpaying citizens and this train goes from one part of the country to another part of the country far away and what's fucked up is that none of these people seem bothered by the excessive heat and none are struggling to breathe or in any real distress so when I say everyone in this train car is dead or appears dead or is about to die because there's no air to breathe it's only partially true because I'm the only one mopping his brow with a damp handkerchief and struggling to breathe with sweat pouring off me and I'm the one in need of rescue and so I wait for Manny or Esperanza to stop this train and board it and then carry me away to safety but what will they want in return is the question because we all know Manny and Esperanza are awful people and everything with them is my left tit for your right tat and I'll show you my quid if you scratch my quo so what I want to know is where is the outrage and the protestors and what time does the revolution start and will it be televised and I enjoy a good uprising as much as anyone just as long as they keep it down and end it early because I have to go to bed soon as I haven't been sleeping well and have a big day tomorrow.

You're Gonna Need My Help Someday

I NEVER HAD A SHOE I cared about except maybe this one pair of boots before the soles wore down thin as paper and I had to throw them out. There was no way to get traction and I'd slip on the ice and fall down hard. This was before I found out that you could re-sole a shoe, that you could take shoes to a cobbler and a day or two later they were fixed.

It's possible those boots meant something because I walked all over the country in them. They never reminded me of my father's boots, which were always mud-soaked and had a pistol tucked deep inside one or the other, which is something I've never done even though I'm American, too.

Today I'm putting on new boots because it's raining, and when I say new I mean less than ten years old. I told Esperanza once that I didn't want to go out in the rain anymore and she said if I found the spaces between drops I'd be fine, that nothing bad would happen. I didn't bother telling her about losing traction and how I slipped on the ice because she was tired of excuses. Then she said something like, umbrellas also work.

This is how Esperanza spoke to me. Once she wanted me to take a class in adult communication, she said I needed the instruction. She'd taken a seminar or two and said it was helpful. Part of her homework was to call people by name, but she made it a point never to practice on me.

I said something like, thousands of years of civilization and this is the best we've come up with, a handheld mushroom-shaped tent. A piece of fabric that yields and crumbles in the wind.

Esperanza didn't know what I was talking about and neither did I, which probably proves her point.

This is when I asked about the rain, if she liked to listen to it at night, if it helped her sleep.

She said she didn't need any help sleeping, that she needed help when she was awake.

I should probably mention we were outside in the rain during this conversation and I couldn't find the spaces between the drops and neither could she.

I asked what does all of this have to do with my shoes, and she answered by walking down the street and never talking to me again.

The Place Is Ringed with Countless Foes

THE GOOD THING about today is I slept through most of it.

What the Man Doesn't Do in the Morning

The man doesn't leave bed when he wakes in the morning, nor does he go to the bathroom to empty his bladder or perform routine ablutions. He doesn't walk into the kitchen to make breakfast. He doesn't retrieve a small bowl from the pantry, doesn't open the refrigerator door to extricate the nonfat yogurt and remove two healthy spoonfuls from the container, then pour a substantial amount of store-bought granola into the bowl. He doesn't cut up strawberries or banana or add roasted unsalted almonds. The man never has cereal for breakfast, either, not the oat cereal he buys at the supermarket nor the oat cereal he buys at the health food store. There is no difference between these cereals other than the price and sugar content, which he doesn't pay attention to even though he'd better start soon. The man needs to start taking care of himself, as he is well into middle age and will likely be dead from a heart attack or colorectal cancer before this decade ends. The man has no almond milk in the refrigerator, nor is there any soy milk or oat milk or rice milk or hemp milk, and certainly not whole milk as the man is lactose intolerant. The man will not make that mistake again, will not test his body to see if perhaps his digestive system has corrected itself and reverted to childhood. The man will not scramble, fry, poach, or boil two or three eggs depending on his appetite. If he were to scramble or fry the eggs, he wouldn't crack the eggs in two so he could separate and then dispose of the yolks in an effort to lower his cholesterol. The man hasn't seen a doctor in years so he doesn't know if he has to watch his cholesterol, though he assumes he should because both his father and grandfather died young of heart attacks, and he will likely suffer the same fate on an August day eight years hence. He'll be unusually tired but will attribute it to not sleeping very well the past week. Then he'll come home from his morning walk to shower. This is where he'll fall. Normally he wouldn't listen to music while in the shower because for years he didn't have a sound system or speaker inside or near the bathroom. But he rectified this two years earlier and would sometimes listen to his favorite country or folk records while he showered. The man will hear the lyrics *there's a hole in Daddy's arm where all the money goes* as his body fails him and he loses consciousness. He will be in the middle of shaving, which is another activity he never engaged in while showering until recently. He couldn't understand why any man would choose to shave in the shower instead of in front of a mirror and over a sink until he tried it once and thought of it as efficient multitasking. He still never masturbated in the shower, as he never liked to masturbate standing up, nor did he make it a practice to urinate in the shower, though he almost always had to urinate. Perhaps he urinated in the shower three or four times in his entire adult life. Instead he stood himself up in the shower and mindlessly rotated his body around and around and let the spray wash over him as he thought about whatever might have troubled his mind. Frequently he thought about death, his own death and the deaths of those he knew, family and friends, but not on this day, as he was concerned about his doubles match tomorrow and whether they could secure a court. This is what he is thinking about as his life concludes, but the man doesn't know this now because how could he. The man is not a fortune teller or seer, so for today he is fine. What he doesn't know about his future is a blessing, as it is to everyone. The man also doesn't know if egg yolks contain cholesterol, if they are more dangerous than the egg whites. He won't slide two pieces of whole wheat or multigrain bread into the toaster, will not spread the Irish butter he enjoys most across the toast. He won't spread any jelly or jam or marmalade or preserves across the toast, either. The man doesn't know if there's a difference between jelly or jam or marmalade or preserves but he suspects there is. He hardly ever prepares steel-cut oats for breakfast and will not measure out how much water is needed according to the ratio on the can. The recommended serving for one is insubstantial and he is unable to figure out how much more to make. He refuses to stand over the stove to stir oatmeal every two or three minutes for half an hour. He never reads a magazine or book while doing this. Never in his life has he made French toast or pancakes or waffles for the effort involved, which seems even greater than preparing steel-cut oats. The man won't do this for himself and he won't do it for his wife or girlfriend, if he's ever had a wife or girlfriend. Years ago he may've had one or two of each and they probably had names like Esperanza and Sofia, but they all insisted on breakfast every morning and this always proved to be problematic for everyone.

The Idea

WE HAD AN IDEA ONCE but it's gone now. The idea concerned a new use for electric fans. This is what happens sometimes. We forget ideas like how we forgot our name. We think our name rhymes with a kind of bird, but we don't know what kind of bird. We don't know anything about birds. Part of the trouble is we're not color blind like other people are color blind. The way other people are color blind is they see a blue bird flying in the wind but it looks green to them. The difference is they know the bird isn't green because they know what they see as green is actually blue. For these people green is blue and blue is green. If you are going to be colorblind, this is the way to do it. We can't see blue or green so all birds look the same. They are all colorless. We've been to the eye doctors but they can't fix us. They say something is wrong with our corneas and they have to cut them out and put in new ones. This sounds awful to us. We don't know why we are meant to suffer like this and neither does the doctor. All we remember is looking around the room one morning and wondering what happened to the walls and carpet. But the walls and carpet aren't important and neither is the doctor who won't help us. What is important is our idea about electric fans.

This idea occurred to us in bed right before we were about to fall asleep and have a bad dream. Every night we have bad dreams. In the dreams people want to kill us because of who we are and what's wrong with us. The bad dreams are always as colorless as the rest of the world, which is why it's all regrettable. We hope maybe to remember our name someday but we don't care too much about it. There is no one here to call us by the name we have ourselves forgotten. Now before we go to bed each night, we try to remember the idea, but we always wind up falling asleep and when we wake we can't think of any use for electric fans other than to plug it into a wall and let it blow all over every colorless thing in the room.

In Time the Savage Bull Doth Bear the Yoke

ONCE ESPERANZA SAID you've got to treat me right day by day and I said get out your little prayer book and get upon your knees to pray because I'm going to leave and you won't see my sweet face no more and then you'll be left to wonder where in the world I've gone.

Into My Own Parade

There were people everywhere like it was a parade. Some of the people were drinking, others laughing and singing. I think it may've been a holiday, something worthy of celebration.

I was out for a walk but had no real destination.

What makes this a story is I was about to be married. My bride's name was Esperanza, and she was supposed to wait for me with the officiate. I told them I had to go check on something, that I'd be right back. I told them to wait here.

She said thank you but I'm ambulatory now.

She was right. A year ago, when I met her, she was bedridden. She'd been in bed her whole life. The sores were the worst part, she said.

This was around the time we sat down and outlined a basic agreement about sex and how we should conduct ourselves. We agreed nothing should slow us down when it comes to sex, not paralysis or coma or death, but then she recovered, which rendered everything null and void.

Now she walks everywhere, to the stores, to the markets, up hills, down aisles.

It's something like a miracle, and everyone knows it. This is when I asked her to marry me again, but another time, when it's more convenient for everyone, when everyone has had a chance to settle down.

I said this as I was walking. She was right behind me the whole time.

I told her I wanted to have her children and raise them to be responsible citizens who held down jobs and paid taxes and contributed to what people call society, but not right now. What I wanted more than anything was to feel domesticated, which she said was paradoxical.

She asked me to come with her to the Irish pub across the street so she could make a counteroffer.

I considered going but got waylaid by the people marching in garish costumes. I had no choice but to fade into my own parade and that's how I ended up.

She couldn't be stopped, though. She kept on walking like it was nothing, like she'd been doing it forever. She never once turned around, looked back. I watched her go until she disappeared into the misty horizon. Everyone in the parade cheered her on.

Every November

EVERY NOVEMBER I WRITE a novel. I start with the first sentence and then I don't stop until it's finished. Once it's finished, I take it out to the backyard and bury it for the squirrels.

I also run the marathon. Sometimes I start but don't finish, sometimes I quit around mile seven because every part of my body hurts and I remember I don't like running.

Every December I stop to rest. I sleep. I go to bed on the first and don't get out of it until Christmas.

Every Christmas I spend alone in a dark room. I think about what I've done in the past year. I think about Jesus. I think about what Jesus has done in the past year. I think about if Jesus ever wrote a novel or ran a marathon.

Come January and the new year, I step outside and look around. I look for Jesus, but he's never on the sidewalk or across the street playing handball with everyone else.

I see everything is the same as it was the year before, so I go back inside.

Chapter Three

THERE IS SO MUCH in the world I can't believe.

Chapter Three

I AM HERE BECAUSE I have been turned in. I have to say it is a relief. I knew something like this was going to happen and I was tired of waiting. And I wanted it to be over, done with. I believe it was Esperanza who turned me in and the reasons she did are numerous. I was almost ready to turn her in, so I cannot blame her for beating me to it. I try not to think of her anymore, so I don't know where she is or what kind of room she is staying in or if she has any plants there to keep her company. I'm not sure what kind of plants I have, though I do know one is a tree. If it's possible to have an indoor palm tree then it might be an indoor palm tree. Trees need water and sunlight, but not too much water, not too much sunlight. The leaves of the tree remind me of palms, though I'm not sure if I've ever seen a palm tree in person. I have seen palms on Palm Sundays when my mother would bring me to church and make me sit quietly and participate in the mass rituals. I remember standing and sitting and kneeling. I never knew when to stand or sit or kneel until others stood, sat, or kneeled first. Then I would follow my mother up to the altar and receive communion. The priest would hold out the wafer and say, body of Christ, and I would say, you're kidding, and the priest would furrow his brow and so I'd cup my hands together to receive it. My mother said, years ago, the priest would place the wafer directly onto your tongue, but I never believed it. Esperanza once fed me grapes while we lounged on a picnic blanket beneath a large oak tree in summer. It was the beginning of our courtship or struggle, which is akin to mincing hairs or splitting words. This is when I learned how she came to this country, smuggled in the trunk of a station wagon, hidden beneath tightly bundled-together packages of cash and cocaine. I was appalled and in love, so I said that must've been awful and you poor thing. I was tickled by her broken English and perfectly shaped toes, each one in proportion to its neighbor. She marveled at what she called my American arrogance.

We talked of matters great and small, of this world and the next. She wasn't religious, although she did wear a gold-plated cross around her neck. It was a gift from her grandmother, and she was told to wear it always. Once I took it in my mouth when she was on top of me and writhing. I remember tonguing each gold-plated plank and her expression when she caught me, something between rapture and repulsion. I think this is how most people take communion, particularly if the priest places the wafer directly into your mouth. Most often I'd palm the wafer and pretend to eat it, and when I was walking back to the pew, I'd slip the wafer into my pants pocket. I was never caught, as no one ever seemed to be watching. The week before Easter is when palms were distributed to parishioners in celebration or remembrance of Jesus' last trip to Jerusalem. I'm not sure this is an event one celebrates because he was about to be tortured and crucified. Some people call it the Passion but that doesn't seem right to me. He rode to town on a donkey and the natives placed palms in his path, for what purpose I can't recall. It makes little sense that it would be for the donkey's benefit. I can't remember if we brought the palms home or left them with the church. They had to burn the leftover palms to use for Ash Wednesday, which was another day our mother brought us to church. I'd always wash my face once we got home, but my mother would walk around all day with the ashes on her forehead. Sometimes I'd see people out in the world like this, with a black smudge on the forehead, walking around like they weren't stained with soot. Add this to the endless list of things I don't understand about people.

I also don't understand the people who monitor me. They say they are trying to help me get better, but all they do is sit on the other side of my window and compile data. They watch me masturbate and conduct experiments, and when I ask for how much longer, they answer by strapping me into a gurney and sedating me. I can never remember my dreams when they sedate me so I don't mind it. I also don't mind the food here, which is better than you'd expect. Yesterday they served paella but I didn't eat the chorizo on account of my acid reflux. They used too much onion and saffron, but it was still enjoyable. I'm not sure what's on the menu for tonight, but I'm hoping it's enchiladas.

I'm trying to make the best of it even though no one listens to me when I talk and they take turns abusing me every day. I imagine I will spend the rest of my life here. Sometimes I wonder if I will die in my sleep or while I'm masturbating or during mealtime. This is why it's best to consider this a last will and testament, and so I tell them to send in a notary public. I tell them I am of sound mind and brutalized body. I leave all my worldly possessions, of which I've few, to the woman in Wyoming or Michigan who stole my wallet and took advantage of my good nature. I tell the notary to wrap up my last will and testament in plastic so it might survive the coming flood. To the rest of you I say this: Stop perpetuating this human folly. Stop with the mindless procreating and inflicting life upon innocents. I cannot go through this again. If nothing else, I want to make that clear.

Of this recent life I can say I was always particular about my appearance, especially my hair. I never did like my hair, as it was thick and unruly, and I could never style it. This is why I decided to shear it all off, which was another reason my parents banished me to the shed and beat me up and down. I remember telling my mother that one day I'd leave and never come back. I told her if you don't think I'm leaving you can count the days I'm gone. She said I didn't have the gumption, which was a word I didn't understand at the time and still don't. I'm not sure if I've ever had gumption, but I am sure I have two large rooms of my own now. This is why I have to pay upfront for three hours of cleaning, because it takes a long time to clean each room properly, and I like for everything to be clean. The people who clean here look like the ones on the other side of the window, meaning they all wear white lab coats and carry clipboards. The only difference is some push mops and buckets around and others carry needles and restraints.

I know it was Esperanza who turned me in and I know I deserve it. I know, too, my mother will never visit me here, and I know Esperanza won't either and neither will Sofia or Tanya or Manny or anyone else from my family, including my father and brothers and the girl I suspected was a sister even though I cannot prove it. They are all of them me and I am all of them too and we are still a family, in spite of all, and maybe even a family of man on an isle of wight, which is something I heard once. Someone was singing it out loud in front of a rapt audience and I've never been able to shake it, something about bombs bursting and comrades weeping and in my mind the Isle of Wight is like the Garden of Eden, if there was a Garden of Eden, which how could there be given the nature of God and man, but that doesn't matter because family is family and there's nothing to be done about it no matter where you are or what you've done, it's all the time inescapable like disappointment and death and I will remain here until then, until I am gone, which I am already, my body and mind all the time bound to Sofia and Tanya and Manny and Esperanza, my puzzle and punishment, all of us spinning in space until we are once and forever gone, and somehow still a family of man on an isle of wight.

About the Author

Robert Lopez is the author of seven other books, including *Good People* and *A Better Class of People*. He lives in Brooklyn and teaches at Stony Brook University.